Frederick Locker-Lampson, Richard Doyle

A Selection from the Works of Frederick Locker

Frederick Locker-Lampson, Richard Doyle

A Selection from the Works of Frederick Locker

ISBN/EAN: 9783337275488

Printed in Europe, USA, Canada, Australia, Japan

Cover: Foto ©Andreas Hilbeck / pixelio.de

More available books at **www.hansebooks.com**

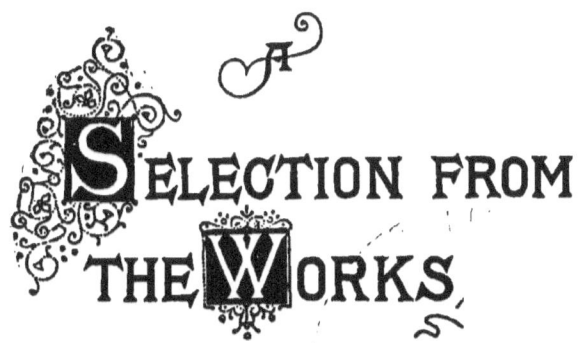

A SELECTION FROM THE WORKS

OF

FREDERICK LOCKER.

WITH ILLUSTRATIONS BY RICHARD DOYLE.

LONDON:

EDWARD MOXON & CO., DOVER STREET.

1865.

PRINTED BY BRADBURY AND EVANS, WHITEFRIARS.
THE ILLUSTRATIONS BY J. E. MILLAIS, R.A., AND RICHARD DOYLE
THE COVER FROM A DESIGN BY JOHN LEIGHTON, F.S.A.
THE SERIES PROJECTED AND SUPERINTENDED BY

SOME of these pieces appeared in a volume called "London Lyrics," of which there have been two editions, the first in 1857, and the second in 1862 ; a few of the pieces have been restored to the reading of the First Edition.

TO C. C. L.

I PAUSE upon the threshold, Charlotte dear,
  To write thy name; so may my book acquire
One golden leaf. For Some yet sojourn here
  Who come and go in homeliest attire,
Unknown, or only by the few who see
  The cross they bear, the good that they have wrought:
Of such art thou, and I have found in thee
  The love and truth that HE, the MASTER, taught;
Thou likest thy humble poet, canst thou say
With truth, dear Charlotte?—"And I like his lay."

ROME, *May*, 1862.

CONTENTS.

	PAGE
THE JESTER'S MORAL	1
BRAMBLE-RISE	6
THE WIDOW'S MITE	10
ON AN OLD MUFF	11
A HUMAN SKULL	15
TO MY GRANDMOTHER	17
O TEMPORA MUTANTUR!	20
REPLY TO A LETTER ENCLOSING A LOCK OF HAIR	22
THE OLD OAK-TREE AT HATFIELD BROADOAK . . .	25
AN INVITATION TO ROME, AND THE REPLY :—	
THE INVITATION	31
THE REPLY	36
OLD LETTERS	40
MY NEIGHBOUR ROSE	43
PICCADILLY	47
THE PILGRIMS OF PALL MALL	50
GERALDINE	53
"O DOMINE DEUS"	56
THE HOUSEMAID	58

viii CONTENTS.

	PAGE
THE OLD GOVERNMENT CLERK	61
A WISH	64
THE JESTER'S PLEA	67
THE OLD CRADLE	70
TO MY MISTRESS	73
TO MY MISTRESS'S BOOTS	75
THE ROSE AND THE RING	78
TO MY OLD FRIEND POSTUMUS	80
THE RUSSET PITCHER	82
THE FAIRY ROSE	87
1863	89
GERALDINE GREEN :—	
I. THE SERENADE	92
II. MY LIFE IS A ——	93
MRS. SMITH	95
THE SKELETON IN THE CUPBOARD	98
THE VICTORIA CROSS	101
ST. GEORGE'S, HANOVER SQUARE	104
SORRENTO	105
JANET	106
BÉRANGER	109
THE BEAR PIT	110
THE CASTLE IN THE AIR	112
GLYCERE	119
VÆ VICTIS	121

CONTENTS.

	PAGE
IMPLORA PACE	123
VANITY FAIR	125
THE LEGENDE OF SIR GYLES GYLES	127
MY FIRST-BORN	133
SUSANNAH :—	
I. THE ELDER TREES	135
II. A KIND PROVIDENCE	137
CIRCUMSTANCE	139
ARCADIA	140
THE CROSSING-SWEEPER	145
A SONG THAT WAS NEVER SUNG	148
MR. PLACID'S FLIRTATION	149
TO PARENTS AND GUARDIANS	154
BEGGARS	157
THE ANGORA CAT	160
ON A PORTRAIT OF DR. LAURENCE STERNE	163
A SKETCH IN SEVEN DIALS	166
LITTLE PITCHER	167
UNFORTUNATE MISS BAILEY	170
ADVICE TO A POET	173
NOTES	177

LIST OF ILLUSTRATIONS.

	PAGE
PORTRAIT OF THE AUTHOR, BY J. E. MILLAIS, R.A.	*To face Title*
THE JESTER	*On Title*
THE JESTER'S MORAL	1
ON AN OLD MUFF	11
THE OLD OAK-TREE AT HATFIELD BROADOAK . .	25
OLD LETTERS	40
PICCADILLY	47
A WISH	64
THE OLD CRADLE	70
TO MY MISTRESS'S BOOTS	75
THE ROSE AND THE RING	78
THE RUSSET PITCHER	82
TAIL PIECE	86
MRS. SMITH	95
THE CASTLE IN THE AIR	112
THE LEGENDE OF SIR GYLES GYLES	127
ARCADIA	140
MR. PLACID'S FLIRTATION	149
THE ANGORA CAT	160
LITTLE PITCHER	167

The JESTERS' MORAL.

I wish that I could run away
  From House, and Court, and Levee:
Where bearded men appear to-day,
  Just Eton boys grown heavy.—W. M. PRAED.

Is human life a pleasant game
  That gives a palm to all?
A fight for fortune, or for fame?
  A struggle, and a fall?
Who views the Past, and all he prized,
  With tranquil exultation?
And who can say, I've realised
  My fondest aspiration?

B

THE JESTER'S MORAL.

Alas, not one ! for rest assured
   That all are prone to quarrel
With Fate, when worms destroy their gourd,
   Or mildew spoils their laurel :
The prize may come to cheer our lot,
   But all too late—and granted
'Tis even better—still 'tis not
   Exactly what we wanted.

My school-boy time ! I wish to praise
   That bud of brief existence,
The vision of my youthful days
   Now trembles in the distance.
An envious vapour lingers here,
   And there I find a chasm ;
But much remains, distinct and clear,
   To sink enthusiasm.

Such thoughts just now disturb my soul
   With reason good—for lately
I took the train to Marley-knoll,
   And crossed the fields to Mately.
I found old Wheeler at his gate,
   Who used rare sport to show me :
My Mentor once on snares and bait—
   But Wheeler did not know me.

"Goodlord!" at last exclaimed the churl,
　"Are you the little chap, sir,
What used to train his hair in curl,
　And wore a scarlet cap, sir?"
And then he fell to fill in blanks,
　And conjure up old faces;
And talk of well-remembered pranks,
　In half forgotten places.

It pleased the man to tell his brief
　And somewhat mournful story,
Old Bliss's school had come to grief—
　And Bliss had "gone to glory."
His trees were felled, his house was razed—
　And what less keenly pained me,
A venerable donkey grazed
　Exactly where he caned me.

And where have all my playmates sped,
　Whose ranks were once so serried?
Why some are wed, and some are dead,
　And some are only buried;
Frank Petre, erst so full of fun,
　Is now St. Blaise's prior—
And Travers, the attorney's son,
　Is member for the shire.

Dame Fortune, that inconstant jade,
   Can smile when least expected,
And those who languish in the shade,
   Need never be dejected.
Poor Pat, who once did nothing right,
   Has proved a famous writer;
While Mat "shirked prayers" (with all his might!)
   And wears, withal, his mitre.

Dull maskers we! Life's festival
   Enchants the blithe new-comer;
But seasons change, and where are all
   These friendships of our summer?
Wan pilgrims flit athwart our track—
   Cold looks attend the meeting—
We only greet them, glancing back,
   Or pass without a greeting!

I owe old Bliss some rubs, but pride
   Constrains me to postpone 'em,
He taught me something, 'ere he died,
   About *nil nisi bonum.*
I've met with wiser, better men,
   But I forgive him wholly;
Perhaps his jokes were sad—but then
   He used to storm so drolly.

I still can laugh, is still my boast,
  But mirth has sounded gayer;
And which provokes my laughter most—
  The preacher, or the player?
Alack, I cannot laugh at what
  Once made us laugh so freely,
For Nestroy and Grassot are not—
  And where is Mr. Keeley?

O, shall I run away from hence,
  And dress and shave like Crusoe?
Or join St. Blaise? No, Common Sense,
  Forbid that I should do so.
I'd sooner dress your Little Miss
  As Paulet shaves his poodles!
As soon propose for Betsy Bliss—
  Or get proposed for Boodle's.

We prate of Life's illusive dyes,
  Yet still fond Hope enchants us;
We all believe we near the prize,
  Till some fresh dupe supplants us!
A bright reward, forsooth! And though
  No mortal has attained it,
I still can hope, for well I know
  That Love has so ordained it.

PARIS, *November*, 1864.

BRAMBLE-RISE.

WHAT changes greet my wistful eyes
In quiet little Bramble-Rise,
  Once smallest of its shire?
How altered is each pleasant nook!
The dumpy church used not to look
  So dumpy in the spire.

This village is no longer mine;
And though the Inn has changed its sign,
  The beer may not be stronger:
The river, dwindled by degrees,
Is now a brook,—the cottages
  Are cottages no longer.

The thatch is slate, the plaster bricks,
The trees have cut their ancient sticks,
  Or else the sticks are stunted:
I'm sure these thistles once grew figs,
These geese were swans, and once these pigs
  More musically grunted.

Where early reapers whistled, shrill
A whistle may be noted still,—
    The locomotive's ravings.
New custom newer want begets,—
My bank of early violets
    Is now a bank for savings!

That voice I have not heard for long!
So Patty still can sing the song
    A merry playmate taught her;
I know the strain, but much suspect
'Tis not the child I recollect,
    But Patty,—Patty's daughter;

And has she too outlived the spells
Of breezy hills and silent dells
    Where childhood loved to ramble?
Then Life was thornless to our ken,
And, Bramble-Rise, thy hills were then
    A rise without a bramble.

Whence comes the change? 'Twere easy told
That some grow wise, and some grow cold,
    And all feel time and trouble:
If Life an empty bubble be,
How sad are those who will not see
    A rainbow in the bubble!

And senseless too, for mistress Fate
Is not the gloomy reprobate
    That mouldy sages thought her;
My heart leaps up, and I rejoice
As falls upon my ear thy voice,
    My frisky little daughter.

Come hither, Pussy, perch on these
Thy most unworthy father's knees,
    And tell him all about it:
Are dolls but bran? Can men be base?
When gazing on thy blessed face
    I'm quite prepared to doubt it.

O, mayst thou own, my winsome elf,
Some day a pet just like thyself,
    Her sanguine thoughts to borrow;
Content to use her brighter eyes,—
Accept her childish ecstacies,—
    If need be, share her sorrow!

The wisdom of thy prattle cheers
This heart; and when outworn in years
    And homeward I am starting,
My Darling, lead me gently down
To Life's dim strand: the dark waves frown,
    But weep not for our parting.

Though Life is called a doleful jaunt,
In sorrow rife, in sunshine scant,
Though earthly joys, the wisest grant,
    Have no enduring basis ;
'Tis something in a desert sere,
For her so fresh—for me so drear,
To find in Puss, my daughter dear,
    A little cool oasis !

APRIL, 1857.

THE WIDOW'S MITE.

THE Widow had but only one,
A puny and decrepit son;
    Yet, day and night,
Though fretful oft, and weak, and small,
A loving child, he was her all—
    The Widow's Mite.

The Widow's might,—yes! so sustained,
She battled onward, nor complained
    When friends were fewer:
And, cheerful at her daily care,
A little crutch upon the stair
    Was music to her.

I saw her then,—and now I see,
Though cheerful and resigned, still she
    Has sorrowed much:
She has—HE gave it tenderly—
Much faith—and, carefully laid by,
    A little crutch.

ON AN OLD MUFF.

TIME has a magic wand!
What is this meets my hand,
Moth-eaten, mouldy, and
     Covered with fluff?
Faded, and stiff, and scant;
Can it be? no, it can't—
Yes,—I declare 'tis Aunt
     Prudence's Muff!

Years ago—twenty-three !
Old Uncle Barnaby
Gave it to Aunty P.—
    Laughing and teasing—
" Pru., of the breezy curls,
Whisper these solemn churls,
What holds a pretty girl's
    Hand without squeezing ? "

Uncle was then a lad
Gay, but, I grieve to add,
Sinful : if smoking bad
    Baccy's a vice :
Glossy was then this mink
Muff, lined with pretty pink
Satin, which maidens think
    " Awfully nice ! "

I see, in retrospect,
Aunt, in her best bedecked,
Gliding, with mien erect,
    Gravely to Meeting :
Psalm-book, and kerchief new,
Peeped from the muff of Pru.—
Young men—and pious too—
    Giving her greeting.

ON AN OLD MUFF.

Pure was the life she led
Then—from this Muff, 'tis said,
Tracts she distributed :—
    Scapegraces many,
Seeing the grace they lacked,
Followed her—one, in fact,
Asked for—and got his tract
    Oftener than any.

Love has a potent spell !
Soon this bold Ne'er-do-well,
Aunt's sweet susceptible
    Heart undermining,
Slipped, so the scandal runs,
Notes in the pretty nun's
Muff—triple-cornered ones—
    Pink as its lining !

Worse even, soon the jade
Fled (to oblige her blade!)
Whilst her friends thought that they'd
    Locked her up tightly :
After such shocking games
Aunt is of wedded dames
Gayest—and now her name's
    Mrs. Golightly.

In female conduct flaw
Sadder I never saw,
Still I've faith in the law
    Of compensation.
Once Uncle went astray—
Smoked, joked, and swore away—
Sworn by, he's now, by a
    Large congregation !

Changed is the Child of Sin,
Now he's (he once was thin)
Grave, with a double chin,—
    Blest be his fat form !
Changed is the garb he wore,—
Preacher was never more
Prized than is Uncle for
    Pulpit or platform.

If all's as best befits
Mortals of slender wits,
Then beg this Muff, and its
    Fair Owner pardon :
All's for the best,—indeed
Such is *my* simple creed—
Still I must go and weed
    Hard in my garden.

A HUMAN SKULL.

A HUMAN skull! I bought it passing cheap,—
  It might be dearer to its first employer;
I thought mortality did well to keep
  Some mute memento of the Old Destroyer.

Time was, some may have prized its blooming skin,
  Here lips were wooed perchance in transport
      tender;—
Some may have chucked what was a dimpled chin,
  And never had my doubt about its gender!

Did she live yesterday or ages back?
  What colour were the eyes when bright and waking?
And were your ringlets fair, or brown, or black,
  Poor little head! that long has done with aching?

It may have held (to shoot some random shots)
  Thy brains, Eliza Fry,—or Baron Byron's,
The wits of Nelly Gwynn, or Doctor Watts,—
  Two quoted bards! two philanthropic sirens!

But this I surely knew before I closed
   The bargain on the morning that I bought it ;
It was not half so bad as some supposed,
   Nor quite as good as many may have thought it.

Who love, can need no special type of death ;
   He bares his awful face too soon, too often ;
" Immortelles " bloom in Beauty's bridal wreath,
   And does not yon green elm contain a coffin ?

O, *cara* mine, what lines of care are these ?
   The heart still lingers with the golden hours,
An Autumn tint is on the chestnut trees,
   And where is all that boasted wealth of flowers ?

If life no more can yield us what it gave,
   It still is linked with much that calls for praises ;
A very worthless rogue may dig the grave,
   But hands unseen will dress the turf with daisies.

TO MY GRANDMOTHER.

(SUGGESTED BY A PICTURE BY MR. ROMNEY.)

THIS relative of mine
Was she seventy and nine
    When she died?
By the canvas may be seen
How she looked at seventeen,—
    As a bride.

Beneath a summer tree
As she sits, her reverie
    Has a charm;
Her ringlets are in taste,—
What an arm! and what a waist
    For an arm!

In bridal coronet,
Lace, ribbons, and *coquette*
    Falbala;
Were Romney's limning true,
What a lucky dog were you,
    Grandpapa!

c

Her lips are sweet as love,—
They are parting !   Do they move ?
    Are they dumb ?—
Her eyes are blue, and beam
Beseechingly, and seem
    To say, " Come."

What funny fancy slips
From atween these cherry lips ?
    Whisper me,
Sweet deity, in paint,
What canon says I mayn't
    Marry thee ?

That good-for-nothing Time
Has a confidence sublime !
    When I first
Saw this lady, in my youth,
Her winters had, forsooth,
    Done their worst.

Her locks (as white as snow)
Once shamed the swarthy crow.
    By-and-by,
That fowl's avenging sprite,
Set his cloven foot for spite
    In her eye.

Her rounded form was lean,
And her silk was bombazine :—
        Well I wot,
With her needles would she sit,
And for hours would she knit,—
        Would she not?

Ah, perishable clay!
Her charms had dropt away
        One by one.
But if she heaved a sigh
With a burthen, it was, " Thy
        Will be done."

In travail, as in tears,
With the fardel of her years
        Overprest,—
In mercy was she borne
Where the weary ones and worn
        Are at rest.

I'm fain to meet you there,—
If as witching as you were,
        Grandmamma!
This nether world agrees
That the better it must please
        Grandpapa.

O TEMPORA MUTANTUR!

YES, here, once more, a traveller,
  I find the Angel Inn,
Where landlord, maids, and serving-men
  Receive me with a grin :
They surely can't remember *me*,
  My hair is grey and scanter ;
I'm changed, so changed since I was here—
  "O tempora mutantur !"

The Angel's not much altered since
  That sunny month of June,
Which brought me here with Pamela
  To spend our honeymoon !
I recollect it down to e'en
  The shape of this decanter,—
We've since been both much put about—
  "O tempora mutantur !"

Ay, there's the clock, and looking-glass
   Reflecting me again ;
She vowed her Love was very fair—
   I see I'm very plain.
And there's that daub of Prince Leeboo :
   'Twas Pamela's fond banter
To fancy it resembled me—
   " O tempora mutantur !"

The curtains have been dyed ; but there,
   Unbroken, is the same,
The very same cracked pane of glass
   On which I scratched her name.
Yes, there's her tiny flourish still,
   It used to so enchant her
To link two happy names in one—
   " O tempora mutantur !"

   *   *   *   *   *

What brought this wanderer here, and why
   Was Pamela away ?
It might be she had found her grave,
   Or he had found her gay.
The fairest fade ; the best of men
   May meet with a supplanter ;—
I wish the times would change their cry
   Of " tempora mutantur."

REPLY TO A LETTER ENCLOSING A LOCK OF HAIR.

" My darling wants to see you soon,"—
I bless the little maid, and thank her;
To do her bidding, night and noon
I draw on Hope—Love's kindest banker!
Old MSS.

If you were false, and if I 'm free,
    I still would be the slave of yore,
Then joined our years were thirty-three,
    And now,—yes now, I 'm thirty-four !
And though you were not learnèd—well,
    I was not anxious you should grow so,—
I trembled once beneath her spell
    Whose spelling was extremely so-so !

Bright season ! why will Memory
    Still haunt the path our rambles took;
The sparrow's nest that made you cry,—
    The lilies captured in the brook.
I lifted you from side to side,
    You seemed as light as that poor sparrow ;
I know who wished it twice as wide,
    I think you thought it rather narrow.

Time was,—indeed, a little while !
   My pony did your heart compel ;
But once, beside the meadow-stile,
   I thought you loved me just as well ;
I kissed your cheek ; in sweet surprise
   Your troubled gaze said plainly, "Should he?"
But doubt soon fled those daisy eyes,—
   " He could not wish to vex me, could he?"

As year succeeds to year, the more
   Imperfect life's fruition seems,
Our dreams, as baseless as of yore,
   Are not the same enchanting dreams.
The girls I love now vote me slow—
   How dull the boys who once seemed witty !
Perhaps I 'm getting old—I know
   I 'm still romantic—more 's the pity !

Ah, vain regret ! to few, perchance,
   Unknown—and profitless to all :
The wisely-gay, as years advance,
   Are gaily-wise. Whate'er befall
We 'll laugh—at folly, whether seen
   Beneath a chimney or a steeple,
At yours, at mine—our own, I mean,
   As well as that of other people.

They cannot be complete in aught,
  Who are not humorously prone,
A man without a merry thought
  Can hardly have a funny-bone!
To say I hate your gloomy men
  Might be esteemed a strong assertion,
If I 've blue devils, now and then,
  I make them dance for my diversion.

And here 's your letter *débonnaire!*
  "*My friend, my dear old friend of yore,*"
And is this curl your daughter's hair?
  I 've seen the Titian tint before.
Are we that pair who used to pass
  Long days beneath the chesnuts shady?
You then were such a pretty lass!—
  I 'm told you 're now as fair a lady.

I 've laughed to hide the tear I shed,
  As when the Jester's bosom swells,
And mournfully he shakes his head,
  We hear the jingle of his bells.
A jesting vein your poet vexed,
  And this poor rhyme, the Fates determine,
Without a parson, or a text,
  Has proved a somewhat prosy sermon.

THE OLD OAK-TREE AT HATFIELD
BROADOAK.

A MIGHTY growth ! The county side
Lamented when the Giant died,
   For England loves her trees :
What misty legends round him cling !
How lavishly he once did fling
   His acorns to the breeze !

To strike a thousand roots in fame,
To give the district half its name,
   The fiat could not hinder;
Last spring he put forth one green bough,—
The red leaves hang there still,—but now
   His very props are tinder.

Elate, the thunderbolt he braved,
Long centuries his branches waved
   A welcome to the blast;
An oak of broadest girth he grew,
And woodman never dared to do
   What Time has done at last.

The monarch wore a leafy crown,
And wolves, ere wolves were hunted down,
   Found shelter at his foot;
Unnumbered squirrels gambolled free,
Glad music filled the gallant tree
   From stem to topmost shoot.

And it were hard to fix the tale
Of when he first peered forth a frail
   Petitioner for dew;
No Saxon spade disturbed his root,
The rabbit spared the tender shoot,
   And valiantly he grew,

And showed some inches from the ground
When Saint Augustine came and found
   Us very proper Vandals:
When nymphs owned bluer eyes than hose,
When England measured men by blows,
   And measured time by candles.

Worn pilgrims blessed his grateful shade
Ere Richard led the first crusade,
   And maidens led the dance   ·
Where, boy and man, in summer-time,
Sweet Chaucer pondered o'er his rhyme ;
   And Robin Hood, perchance,

Stole hither to maid Marian,
(And if they did not come, one can
   At any rate suppose it);
They met beneath the mistletoe,—
We did the same, and ought to know
   The reason why they chose it.

And this was called the traitor's branch,—
Stern Warwick hung six yeomen stanch
   Along its mighty fork ;
Uncivil wars for them !   The fair
Red rose and white still bloom,—but where
   Are Lancaster and York ?

Right mournfully his leaves he shed
To shroud the graves of England's dead,
  By English falchion slain ;
And cheerfully, for England's sake,
He sent his kin to sea with Drake,
  When Tudor humbled Spain.

A time-worn tree, he could not bring
His heart to screen the merry king,
  Or countenance his scandals ;—
Then men were measured by their wit,—
And then the mimic statesmen lit
  At either end their candles !

While Blake was busy with the Dutch
They gave his poor old arms a crutch :
  And thrice four maids and men ate
A meal within his rugged bark,
When Coventry bewitched the park,
  And Chatham swayed the senate.

His few remaining boughs were green,
And dappled sunbeams danced between,
  Upon the dappled deer,
When, clad in black, a pair were met
To read the Waterloo Gazette,—
  They mourned their darling here.

They joined their boy.　The tree at last
Lies prone—discoursing of the past,
　　Some fancy-dreams awaking;
Resigned, though headlong changes come,—
Though nations arm to tuck of drum,
　　And dynasties are quaking.

Romantic spot!　By honest pride
Of eld tradition sanctified;
　　My pensive vigil keeping,
I feel thy beauty like a spell,
And thoughts, and tender thoughts, upwell,
　　That fill my heart to weeping.
　　　　*　　*　　*　　*　　*
The Squire affirms, with gravest look,
His oak goes up to Domesday Book!—
　　And some say even higher!
We rode last week to see the ruin,
We love the fair domain it grew in,
　　And well we love the Squire.

A nature loyally controlled,
And fashioned in that righteous mould
　　Of English gentleman;—
My child may some day read these rhymes,—
She loved her "godpapa" betimes,—
　　The little Christian!

I love the Past, its ripe pleasànce,
Its lusty thought, and dim romance,
   And heart-compelling ditties ;
But more, these ties, in mercy sent,
With faith and true affection blent,
And, wanting them, I were content
   To murmur, " *Nunc dimittis.*"

HALLINGBURY, *April,* 1859.

AN INVITATION TO ROME, AND THE REPLY.

THE INVITATION.

O, COME to Rome, it is a pleasant place,
  Your London sun is here seen shining brightly :
The Briton too puts on a cheery face,
  And Mrs. Bull is *suave* and even sprightly.
The Romans are a kind and cordial race,
  The women charming, if one takes them rightly ;
I see them at their doors, as day is closing,
More proud than duchesses—and more imposing.

A "*far niente*" life promotes the graces ;—
  They pass from dreamy bliss to wakeful glee,
And in their bearing, and their speech, one traces
  A breadth of grace and depth of courtesy
That are not found in more inclement places ;
  Their clime and tongue seem much in harmony ;
The Cockney met in Middlesex, or Surrey,
Is often cold—and always in a hurry.

Though "*far niente*" is their passion, they
  Seem here most eloquent in things most slight;
No matter what it is they have to say,
  The manner always sets the matter right.
And when they've plagued or pleased you all the day
  They sweetly wish you "a most happy night."
Then, if they fib, and if their stories tease you,
'Tis always something that they've wished to please you.

O, come to Rome, nor be content to read
  Alone of stately palaces and streets
Whose fountains ever run with joyous speed,
  And never-ceasing murmur.   Here one meets
Great Memnon's monoliths—or, gay with weed,
  Rich capitals, as corner stones, or seats—
The sites of vanished temples, where now moulder
Old ruins, hiding ruin even older.

Ay, come, and see the pictures, statues, churches,
  Although the last are commonplace, or florid.
Some say 'tis here that superstition perches,—
  Myself I'm glad the marbles have been quarried.
The sombre streets are worthy your researches:
  The ways are foul, the lava pavement's horrid,
But pleasant sights, which squeamishness disparages,
Are missed by all who roll about in carriages.

About one fane I deprecate all sneering,
  For during Christmas-time I went there daily,
Amused, or edified—or both—by hearing
  The little preachers of the *Ara Cæli*.
Conceive a four-year-old *bambina* rearing
  Her small form on a rostrum, tricked out gaily,
And lisping, what for doctrine may be frightful,
With action quite dramatic and delightful.

O come ! We'll charter such a pair of nags !
  The country's better seen when one is riding :
We'll roam where yellow Tiber speeds or lags
  At will. The aqueducts are yet bestriding
With giant march (now whole, now broken crags
  With flowers plumed) the swelling and subsiding
Campagna, girt by purple hills, afar—
That melt in light beneath the evening star.

A drive to Palestrina will be pleasant—
  The wild fig grows where erst her turrets stood ;
There oft, in goat-skins clad, a sun-burnt peasant
  Like Pan comes frisking from his ilex wood,
And seems to wake the past time in the present.
  Fair *contadina*, mark his mirthful mood,
No antique satyr he. The nimble fellow
Can join with jollity your *Salterello*.

D

Old sylvan peace and liberty !   The breath
   Of life to unsophisticated man.
Here Mirth may pipe, here Love may weave his wreath,
   " Per dar' al mio bene."   When you can,
Come share their leafy solitudes.   Grim Death
   And Time are grudging of Life's little span :
Wan Time speeds swiftly o'er the waving corn,
Death grins from yonder cynical old thorn.

I dare not speak of Michael Angelo—
   Such theme were all too splendid for my pen.
And if I breathe the name of Sanzio
   (The brightest of Italian gentlemen),
It is that love casts out my fear—and so
   I claim with him a kindredship.   Ah ! when
We love, the name is on our hearts engraven,
As is thy name, my own dear Bard of Avon !

Nor is the Colosseum theme of mine,
   'Twas built for poet of a larger daring ;
The world goes there with torches—I decline
   Thus to affront the moonbeams with their flaring.
Some time in May our forces we'll combine
   (Just you and I) and try a midnight airing,
And then I'll quote this rhyme to you—and then
You'll muse upon the vanity of men.

O come—I send a leaf of tender fern,
　'Twas plucked where Beauty lingers round decay :
The ashes buried in a sculptured urn
　Are not more dead than Rome—so dead to-day !
That better time, for which the patriots yearn,
　Enchants the gaze, again to fade away.
They wait and pine for what is long denied,
And thus I wait till thou art by my side.

Thou'rt far away !　Yet, while I write, I still
　Seem gently, Sweet, to press thy hand in mine ;
I cannot bring myself to drop the quill,
　I cannot yet thy little hand resign !
The plain is fading into darkness chill,
　The Sabine peaks are flushed with light divine,
I watch alone, my fond thought wings to thee,
O come to Rome—O come, O come to me !

THE REPLY.

DEAR Exile, I was pleased to get
    Your rhymes, I laid them up in cotton ;
You know that you are all to " Pet,"
    I feared that I was quite forgotten :
Mama, who scolds me when I mope,
    Insists—and she is wise as gentle—
That I am still in love—I hope
    That you are rather sentimental.

Perhaps you think a child should not
    Be gay unless her slave is with her ;
Of course you love old Rome, and, what
    Is more, would like to coax me thither :
What ! quit this dear delightful maze
    Of calls and balls, to be intensely
Discomfited in fifty ways—
    I like your confidence immensely !

Some girls who love to ride and race,
    And live for dancing—like the Bruens,
Confess that Rome's a charming place,
    In spite of all the stupid ruins:

I think it might be sweet to pitch
    One's tent beside those banks of Tiber,
And all that sort of thing—of which
    Dear Hawthorne's "quite" the best describer.

To see stone pines, and marble gods,
    In garden alleys—red with roses—
The Perch where Pio Nono nods;
    The Church where Raphael reposes.
Make pleasant *giros*—when we may;
    Jump *stagionate*—where they're easy;
And play croquet—the Bruens say
    There's turf behind the *Ludovisi*.

I'll bring my books, though Mrs. Mee
    Says packing books is such a worry;
I'll bring my " Golden Treasury,"
    Manzoni—and, of course, a "Murray;"
A TUPPER, whom you men despise;
    A Dante—Auntie owns a quarto—
I'll try and buy a smaller size,
    And read him on the *muro torto*.

But can I go? *La Madre* thinks
    It would be such an undertaking :—
I wish we could consult a sphynx;—
    The thought alone has set her quaking.

Papa—we do not mind Papa—
   Has got some "notice" of some "motion,"
And could not stay; but, why not,—Ah,
   I've not the very slightest notion.

The Browns have come to stay a week,
   They've brought the boys, I haven't thanked 'em,
For Baby *Grand*, and Baby *Pic*,
   Are playing cricket in my sanctum:
Your Rover too affects my den,
   And when I pat the dear old whelp, it . .
It makes me think of you, and then . .
   And then I cry—I cannot help it.

Ah, yes—before you left me, ere
   Our separation was impending,
These eyes had seldom shed a tear—
   For mine was joy that knew no ending;
Yes, soon there came a change, too soon:
   The first faint cloud that rose to grieve me
Was knowledge I possessed the boon,
   And then a fear such bliss might leave me.

This strain is sad: yet, understand,
   Your words have made my spirit better:
And when I first took pen in hand,
   I meant to write a cheery letter;

But skies were dull,—Rome sounded hot,
    I fancied I could live without it :
I thought I'd go—I thought I'd not,
    And then I thought I'd think about it.

The sun now glances o'er the Park,
    If tears are on my cheek, they glitter ;
I think I've kissed your rhymes, for—hark !
    My "bulley" gives a saucy twitter.
Your blessed words extinguish doubt,
    A sudden breeze is gaily blowing,
And, hark ! The minster bells ring out—
    "She ought to go ! Of course she's going."

OLD LETTERS.

OLD letters ! wipe away the tear
  For vows and hopes so vainly worded ?
A pilgrim finds his journal here
  Since first his youthful loins were girded.

Yes, here are wails from Clapham Grove,
  How could philosophy expect us

To live with Dr. Wise, and love
   Rice pudding and the Greek Delectus?

Explain why childhood's path is sown
   With moral and scholastic tin-tacks;
Ere sin original was known,
   Did Adam groan beneath the syntax?

How strange to parley with the dead!
   Keep ye your green, wan leaves? How many
From Friendship's tree untimely shed!
   And here is one as sad as any;

A ghastly bill! "I disapprove,"
   And yet She help'd me to defray it—
What tokens of a Mother's love!
   O, bitter thought! I can't repay it.

And here's the offer that I wrote
   In '33 to Lucy Diver;
And here John Wylie's begging note,—
   He never paid me back a stiver.

And here my feud with Major Spike,
   Our bet about the French Invasion;

I must confess I acted like
    A donkey upon that occasion.

Here's news from Paternoster Row!
    How mad I was when first I learnt it:
They would not take my Book, and now
    I'd give a trifle to have burnt it.

And here a pile of notes, at last,
    With " love," and " dove," and " sever," " never,"—
Though hope, though passion may be past,
    Their perfume is as sweet as ever.

A human heart should beat for two,
    Despite the scoffs of single scorners;
And all the hearths I ever knew
    Had got a pair of chimney corners.

See here a double violet—
    Two locks of hair—a deal of scandal;
I'll burn what only brings regret—
    Go, Betty, fetch a lighted candle.

MY NEIGHBOUR ROSE.

THOUGH slender walls our hearths divide,
No word has passed from either side,
Your days, red-lettered all, must glide
　　Unvexed by labour :
I've seen you weep, and could have wept ;
I've heard you sing, and may have slept ;
Sometimes I hear your chimneys swept,
　　My charming neighbour !

Your pets are mine.　Pray what may ail
The pup, once eloquent of tail ?
I wonder why your nightingale
　　Is mute at sunset !
Your puss, demure and pensive, seems
Too fat to mouse.　She much esteems
Yon sunny wall—and sleeps and dreams
　　Of mice she once ate.

Our tastes agree.   I doat upon
Frail jars, turquoise and celadon,
The "Wedding March" of Mendelssohn,
　　And *Penseroso*.　　.
When sorely tempted to purloin
Your *pietà* of Marc Antoine,
Fair Virtue doth fair play enjoin,
　　Fair Virtuoso !

At times an Ariel, cruel-kind,
Will kiss my lips, and stir your blind,
And whisper low, "She hides behind ;
　　Thou art not lonely."
The tricksy sprite did erst assist
At hushed Verona's moonlight tryst ;
Sweet Capulet ! thou wert not kissed
　　By light winds only.

I miss the simple days of yore,
When two long braids of hair you wore,
And *chat botté* was wondered o'er,
　　In corner cosy.
But gaze not back for tales like those :
'Tis all in order, I suppose,
The Bud is now a blooming ROSE,—
　　A rosy posy !

Indeed, farewell to bygone years ;
How wonderful the change appears—
For curates now and cavaliers
  In turn perplex you :
The last are birds of feather gay,
Who swear the first are birds of prey ;
I'd scare them all had I my way,
  But that might vex you.

At times I've envied, it is true,
That joyous hero, twenty-two,
Who sent *bouquets* and *billets-doux*,
  And wore a sabre.
The rogue ! how tenderly he wound
His arm round one who never frowned ;
He loves you well.   Now, is he bound
  To love *my* neighbour ?

The bells are ringing.   As is meet,
White favours fascinate the street,
Sweet faces greet me, rueful-sweet
  'Twixt tears and laughter :
They crowd the door to see her go—
The bliss of one brings many woe—
Oh ! kiss the bride, and I will throw
  The old shoe after.

What change in one short afternoon,—
My Charming Neighbour gone,—so soon!
Is yon pale orb her honey-moon
    Slow rising hither?
O lady, wan and marvellous,
How often have we communed thus;
Sweet memories shall dwell with us,
    And joy go with her!

PICCADILLY.

Piccadilly !—shops, palaces, bustle, and breeze,
The whirring of wheels, and the murmur of trees,
By daylight, or nightlight,—or noisy, or stilly,—
Whatever my mood is—I love Piccadilly.

Wet nights, when the gas on the pavement is streaming,
And young Love is watching, and old Love is dreaming,
And Beauty is whirled off to conquest, where shrilly
Cremona makes nimble thy toes, Piccadilly !

Bright days, when we leisurely pace to and fro,
And meet all the people we do or don't know,—
Here is jolly old Brown, and his fair daughter Lillie ;
—No wonder, young pilgrim, you like Piccadilly !

See yonder pair riding, how fondly they saunter !
She smiles on her poet, whose heart's in a canter :
Some envy her spouse, and some covet her filly,
He envies them both,—he's an ass, Piccadilly !

Now were I that gay bride, with a slave at my feet,
I would choose me a house in my favourite street ;
Yes or no—I would carry my point, willy, nilly,
If " no,"—pick a quarrel, if " yes,"—Piccadilly !

From Primrose balcony, long ages ago,
" Old Q " sat at gaze,—who now passes below ?
A frolicsome Statesman, the Man of the Day,
A laughing philosopher, gallant and gay ;
No hero of story more manfully trod,
Full of years, full of fame, and the world at his nod,
Heu, anni fugaces !   The wise and the silly,—
Old P or old Q,—we must quit Piccadilly.

Life is chequered,—a patchwork of smiles and of frowns ;
We value its ups, let us muse on its downs ;

There's a side that is bright, it will then turn us
    t'other,—
One turn, if a good one, deserves such another.
These downs are delightful, *these* ups are not hilly,—
Let us turn one more turn ere we quit Piccadilly.

THE PILGRIMS OF PALL MALL.

My little friend, so small and neat,
Whom years ago I used to meet
    In Pall Mall daily ;
How cheerily you tripped away
To work, it might have been to play,
    You tripped so gaily.

And Time trips too. This moral means
You then were midway in the teens
    That I was crowning ;
We never spoke, but when I smiled
At morn or eve, I know, dear Child,
    You were not frowning.

Each morning when we met, I think
Some sentiment did us two link—
    Nor joy, nor sorrow ;
And then at eve, experience-taught,
Our hearts returned upon the thought,—
    We meet to-morrow !

And you were poor; and how?—and why?
How kind to come! it was for my
    Especial grace meant!
Had you a chamber near the stars,
A bird,—some treasured plants in jars,
    About your casement?

I often wander up and down,
When morning bathes the silent town
    In golden glory:
Perchance, unwittingly, I've heard
Your thrilling-toned canary-bird
    From some third story.

I've seen great changes since we met;—
A patient little seamstress yet,
    With small means striving,
Have you a Lilliputian spouse?
And do you dwell in some doll's house?
    —Is baby thriving?

Can bloom like thine—my heart grows chill—
Have sought that bourne unwelcome still
    To bosom smarting?
The most forlorn—what worms we are!—
Would wish to finish this cigar
    Before departing.

Sometimes I to Pall Mall repair,
And see the damsels passing there ;
    But if I try to
Obtain one glance, they look discreet,
As though they'd some one else to meet ;—
    As have not *I* too?

Yet still I often think upon
Our many meetings, come and gone !
    July—December !
Now let us make a tryst, and when,
Dear little soul, we meet again,—
The mansion is preparing—then
    Thy Friend remember !

GERALDINE.

THIS simple child has claims
On your sentiment—her name's
　　　Geraldine.
Be tender—but beware,
For she's frolicsome as fair,
　　　And fifteen.

She has gifts that have not cloyed,
For these gifts she has employed,
　　　And improved :
She has bliss which lives and leans
Upon loving—and that means
　　　She is loved.

She has grace.　A grace refined
By sweet harmony of mind :
　　　And the Art,
And the blessed Nature, too,
Of a tender, and a true
　　　Little heart.

And yet I must not vault
Over any little fault
          That she owns :
Or others might rebel,
And might enviously swell
          In their zones.

She is tricksy as the fays,
Or her pussy when it plays
          With a string :
She's a goose about her cat,
And her ribbons—and all that
          Sort of thing.

These foibles are a blot,
Still she never can do what
          Is not nice,
Such as quarrel, and give slaps—
As I've known her get, perhaps,
          Once or twice.

The spells that move her soul
Are subtle—sad or droll—
          She can show
That virtuoso whim
Which consecrates our dim
          Long-ago.

A love that is not sham
For Stothard, Blake, and Lamb ;
  And I've known
Cordelia's sad eyes
Cause angel-tears to rise
  In her own.

Her gentle spirit yearns
When she reads of Robin Burns—
  Luckless Bard !
Had she blossomed in thy time,
How rare had been the rhyme
  —And reward !

Thrice happy then is he
Who, planting such a Tree,
  Sees it bloom
To shelter him—indeed
We have sorrow as we speed
  To our doom !

I am happy having grown
Such a Sapling of my own ;
  And I crave
No garland for my brows,
But peace beneath its boughs
  Till the grave.

> " O DOMINE DEUS,
>   SPERAVI IN TE,
>   O CARE MI JESU,
>   NUNC LIBERA ME."

HER quiet resting-place is far away,
  None dwelling there can tell you her sad story :
The stones are mute.   The stones could only say,
  "A humble spirit passed away to glory."

She loved the murmur of this mighty town,
  The lark rejoiced her from its lattice prison ;
A streamlet soothes her now,—the bird has flown,—
  Some dust is waiting there—a soul has risen.

No city smoke to stain the heather bells,—
  Sigh, gentle winds, around my lone love sleeping,—
She bore her burthen here, but now she dwells
  Where scorner never came, and none are weeping.

O cough ! O cruel cough ! O gasping breath !
  These arms were round my darling at the latest :
All scenes of death are woe—but painful death
  In those we dearly love is surely greatest !

I could not die. He willed it otherwise ;
  My lot is here, and sorrow, wearing older,
Weighs down the heart, but does not fill the eyes,
  And even friends may think that I am colder.

I might have been more kind, more tender ; now
  Repining wrings my bosom. I am grateful
No eye can see this mark upon my brow,
  Yet even gay companionship is hateful.

But when at times I steal away from these,
  And find her grave, and pray to be forgiven,
And when I watch beside her on my knees,
  I think I am a little nearer heaven.

THE HOUSEMAID.

"Bright volumes of vapour through Lothbury glide."

ALONE she sits, with air resigned
She watches by the window-blind :
    Poor girl !   No doubt
The pilgrims here despise thy lot :
Thou canst not stir—because 'tis not
    Thy *Sunday out.*

To play a game of hide and seek
With dust and cobwebs all the week,
    Small pleasure yields :
O dear, how nice it is to drop
One's scrubbing-brush, one's pail and mop—
    And scour the fields !

Poor Bodies some such Sundays know ;
They seldom come.   How soon they go !
    But Souls can roam.
And, lapt in visions airy-sweet,
She sees in this too doleful street
    Her own loved Home !

The road is now no road.   She pranks
A brawling stream with thymy banks ;
    In Fancy's realm
This post sustains no lamp—aloof
It spreads above her parents' roof
    A gracious elm.

How often has she valued there
A father's aid—a mother's care :—
    She now has neither :
And yet—such work in dreams is done,
She still may sit and smile with one
    More dear than either.

The poor can love through woe and pain,
Although their homely speech is fain
    To halt in fetters :
They feel as much, and do far more
Than those, at times of meaner ore,
    Miscalled *their Betters*.

Sometimes, on summer afternoons
Of sundry sunny Mays and Junes—
    Meet Sunday weather,
I pass her window by design,
And wish her *Sunday out* and mine
    Might fall together.

For sweet it were my lot to dower
With one brief joy, one white-robed flower;
    And prude, or preacher,
Could hardly deem it much amiss
To lay one on the path of this
    Forlorn young creature.

Yet if her thought on wooing runs—
And if her swain and she are ones
    Who fancy strolling,
She'd like my nonsense less than his,
And so it's better as it is—
    And that's consoling.

Her dwelling is unknown to fame—
Perchance she's fair—perchance her name
    Is *Car*, or *Kitty;*
She may be *Jane*—she might be plain—
For need the object of one's strain
    Be always pretty?

THE OLD GOVERNMENT CLERK.

WE knew an old Scribe, it was "once on a time,"—
   An era to set sober datists despairing ;—
Then let them despair ! Darby sat in a chair
   Near the Cross that gave name to the village of
     Charing.

Though silent and lean, Darby was not malign,—
   What hair he had left was more silver than sable ;—
He had also contracted a curve in his spine
   From bending too constantly over a table.

His pay and expenditure, quite in accord,
   Were both on the strictest economy founded ;
His masters were known as the Sealing-wax Board,
   Who ruled where red tape and snug places abounded.

In his heart he looked down on this dignified knot,—
   For why, the forefather of one of these senators,
A rascal concerned in the Gunpowder Plot,
   Had been barber-surgeon to Darby's progenitors.

Poor fool! Life is all a vagary of Luck,—
  Still, for thirty long years of genteel destitution
He'd been writing State Papers, which means he had
      stuck
    Some heads and some tails to much circumlocution.

This sounds rather weary and dreary; but, no!
  Though strictly inglorious, his days were quiescent,
His red-tape was tied in a true-lover's bow
    Each night when returning to Rosemary Crescent.

There Joan meets him smiling, the young ones are
      there,
  His coming is bliss to the half-dozen wee things;
Of his advent the dog and the cat are aware,
    And Phyllis, neat-handed, is laying the tea-things.

East wind! sob eerily! sing, kettle! cheerily!
  Baby's abed,—but its father will rock it;
Little ones boast your permission to toast
    The cake that good fellow brought home in his
      pocket.

This greeting the silent old Clerk understands,—
  His friends he can love, had he foes, he could
      mock them;

So met, so surrounded, his bosom expands,—
  Some tongues have more need of such scenes to
    unlock them.

And Darby, at least, is resigned to his lot,
  And Joan, rather proud of the sphere he's adorning,
Has well-nigh forgotten that Gunpowder Plot,
  And *he* won't recall it till ten the next morning.

A kindly good man, quite a stranger to fame,
  His heart still is green, though his head shows a
    hoar lock ;
Perhaps his particular star is to blame,—
  It may be, he never took time by the forelock.

A day must arrive when, in pitiful case,
  He will drop from his Branch, like a fruit more than
    mellow ;
Is he yet to be found in his usual place ?
  Or is he already forgotten, poor fellow ?

If still at his duty he soon will arrive,—
  He passes this turning because it is shorter,—
If not within sight as the clock's striking five,
  We shall see him before it is chiming the quarter.

A WISH.

To the south of the church, and beneath yonder yew,
    A pair of child-lovers I've seen ,
More than once were they there, and the years of the two,
    When added, might number thirteen.

They sat on the grave that has never a stone
    The name of the dead to determine,

It was Life paying Death a brief visit—alone
  A notable text.for a sermon.

They tenderly prattled ; what was it they said ?
  The turf on that hillock was new ;
Dear Little Ones, did ye know aught of the Dead,
  Or could he be heedful of you ?

I wish to believe, and believe it I must,
  Her father beneath them was laid :
I wish to believe,—I will take it on trust,
  That father knew all that they said.

My own, you are five, very nearly the age
  Of that poor little fatherless child :
And some day a true-love your heart will engage,
  When on earth I my last may have smiled.

Then visit my grave, like a good little lass,
  Where'er it may happen to be,
And if any daisies should peer through the grass,
  Be sure they are kisses from me.

And place not a stone to distinguish my name,
  For strangers to see and discuss :

F

But come with your lover, as these lovers came,
   And talk to him sweetly of *us*.

And while you are smiling, your father will smile
   Such a dear little daughter to have,
But mind,—O yes, mind you are happy the while—
   I wish you to visit my Grave.

THE JESTER'S PLEA.

These verses were published in 1862, in a volume of Poems (by several hands), entitled "An Offering to Lancashire."

THE World! Was jester ever in
    A viler than the present?
Yet if it ugly be—as sin,
    It almost is—as pleasant!
It is a merry world (*pro tem.*)
    And some are gay, and therefore
It pleases them—but some condemn
    The fun they do not care for.

It is an ugly world. Offend
    Good people—how they wrangle!
The manners that they never mend!
    The characters they mangle!
They eat, and drink, and scheme, and plod,
    And go to church on Sunday—
And many are afraid of God—
    And more of *Mrs. Grundy.*

F 2

The time for Pen and Sword was when
    " My ladye fayre," for pity
Could tend her wounded knight, and then
    Grow tender at his ditty !
Some ladies now make pretty songs,—
    And some make pretty nurses :—
Some men are good for righting wrongs,—
    And some for writing verses.

I wish We better understood
    The tax that poets levy !—
I know the Muse is very *good*—
    I think she's rather heavy:
She now compounds for winning ways
    By morals of the sternest—
Methinks the lays of now-a-days
    Are painfully in earnest.

When Wisdom halts, I humbly try
    To make the most of Folly :
If Pallas be unwilling, I
    Prefer to flirt with Polly,—
To quit the goddess for the maid
    Seems low in lofty musers—
But Pallas is a haughty jade—
    And beggars can't be choosers.

I do not wish to see the slaves
  Of party, stirring passion,
Or psalms quite superseding staves,
  Or piety "the fashion."
I bless the Hearts where pity glows,
  Who, here together banded,
Are holding out a hand to those
  That wait so empty-handed!

A righteous Work!—My Masters, may
  A Jester by confession,
Scarce noticed join, half sad, half gay,
  The close of your procession?
The motley here seems out of place
  With graver robes to mingle,
But if one tear bedews his face,
  Forgive the bells their jingle.

THE OLD CRADLE.

And this was your Cradle? why, surely, my Jenny,
    Such slender dimensions go somewhat to show
You were a delightfully small Pic-a-ninny
    Some nineteen or twenty short summers ago.

Your baby-days flowed in a much-troubled channel;
    I see you as then in your impotent strife,
A tight little bundle of wailing and flannel,
    Perplexed with that newly-found fardel called Life.

To hint at an infantine frailty is scandal ;
 Let bygones be bygones—and somebody knows
It was bliss such a Baby to dance and to dandle,
 Your cheeks were so velvet—so rosy your toes.

Ay, here is your Cradle, and Hope, a bright spirit,
 With Love now is watching beside it, I know.
They guard the small nest you yourself did inherit
 Some nineteen or twenty short summers ago.

It is Hope gilds the future,—Love welcomes it
  smiling ;
 Thus wags this old world, therefore stay not to ask—
" My future bids fair, is my future beguiling ? "
 If masked, still it pleases—then raise not the mask.

Is Life a poor coil some would gladly be doffing ?
 He is riding post-haste who their wrongs will adjust ;
For at most 'tis a footstep from cradle to coffin—
 From a spoonful of pap to a mouthful of dust.

Then smile as your future is smiling, my Jenny !
 Though blossoms of promise are lost in the rose,
I still see the face of my small Pic-a-ninny
  Unchanged, for these cheeks are as blooming as
  those.

Ay, here is your Cradle ! much, much to my liking,
　　Though nineteen or twenty long winters have sped ;
But, hark ! as I'm talking there's six o'clock striking,
　　It is time JENNY'S BABY should be in its bed !

TO MY MISTRESS.

O COUNTESS, each succeeding year
Reveals that Time is wasting here:
He soon will do his worst by you,
And garner all your roses too !

It pleases Time to fold his wings
Around our best and brightest things ;
He'll mar your damask cheek, as now
He stamps his mark upon my brow.

The same mute planets rise and shine
To rule your days and nights as mine,
I once was young as you,— and see . . !
You some day will be old as me.

And yet I bear a mighty charm
Which shields me from your worst alarm ;
And bids me gaze, with front sublime,
On all these ravages of Time.

You boast a charm that all would prize,
This gift of mine, which you despise,
May, like enough, still hold its sway
When all your boast has passed away.

My charm may long embalm the lures
Of eyes, as sweet to me as yours:
And ages hence the great and good
Will judge you as I choose they should.

In days to come the count or clown,
With whom I still shall win renown,
Will only know that you were fair
Because I chanced to say you were.

Fair Countess—I wax grey—awhile
Your youthful swains will sigh or smile;
But should you scorn, for smile or sigh,
A grey old Bard—as great as I?

KENWOOD, *July* 21, 1864.

MY MISTRESS'S BOOTS.

THEY nearly strike me dumb,
And I tremble when they come
    Pit-a-pat :
This palpitation means
That these boots are Geraldine's—
    Think of that !

Oh, where did hunter win
So delicate a skin
    For her feet ?

You lucky little kid,
You perished, so you did,
    For my sweet.

The faery stitching gleams
On the toes, and in the seams,
    And reveals
That Pixies were the wags
Who tipped these funny tags,
    And these heels.

What soles! so little worn!
Had Crusoe—soul forlorn!—
    Chanced to view
One printed near the tide,
How hard he would have tried
    For the two!

For Gerry's debonair,
And innocent, and fair
    As a rose:
She's an angel in a frock,
With a fascinating cock
    To her nose.

Those simpletons who squeeze
Their extremities to please
    Mandarins,

Would positively flinch
From venturing to pinch
    Geraldine's.

Cinderella's *lefts and rights*
To Geraldine's were frights :
    And, in truth,
The damsel, deftly shod,
Has dutifully trod
    From her youth.

The mansion—ay, and more,
The cottage of the poor,
    Where there's grief,
Or sickness, are her choice—
And the music of her voice
    Brings relief.

Come, Gerry, since it suits
Such a pretty Puss-in-Boots
    These to don,
Set your little hand awhile
On my shoulder, dear, and I'll
    Put them on.

ALBURY, *June 29, 1864.*

THE ROSE AND THE RING.

(Christmas 1854, and Christmas 1863.)

SHE smiles—but her heart is in sable,
    And sad as her Christmas is chill:
She reads, and her book is the fable
    He penned for her while she was ill.
It is nine years ago since he wrought it
    Where reedy old Tiber is king,
And chapter by chapter he brought it—
    And read her the Rose and the Ring.

And when it was printed, and gaining
   Renown with all lovers of glee,
He sent her this copy containing
   His comical little *croquis;*
A sketch of a rather droll couple—
   She's pretty—he's quite t'other thing!
He begs (with a spine vastly supple)
   She will study the Rose and the Ring.

It pleased the kind Wizard to send her
   The last and the best of his toys,
His heart had a sentiment tender
   For innocent women and boys:
And though he was great as a scorner,
   The guileless were safe from his sting,—
How sad is past mirth to the mourner!—
   A tear on the Rose and the Ring!

She reads—I may vainly endeavour
   Her mirth-chequered grief to pursue;
For she hears she has lost—and for ever—
   A Heart that was known by so few;
But I wish on the shrine of his glory
   One fair little blossom to fling;
And you see there's a nice little story
   Attached to the Rose and the Ring!

ᶦᴸ TO MY OLD FRIEND POSTUMUS.

(J. G.)

My Friend, our few remaining years
  Are hasting to an end,
They glide away, and lines are here
  That time will never mend ;
Thy blameless life avails thee not,—
  Alas, my dear old Friend !

From mother Earth's green orchard trees
  The fairest fruit is blown,
The lad was gay who slumbers near,
  The lass he loved is gone ;
Death lifts the burthen from the poor,
  And will not spare the throne.

And vainly are we fenced about
  From peril, day and night,
The awful rapids must be shot,
  Our shallop is but slight ;
So pray, when parting, we descry
  A cheering beacon-light.

O pleasant Earth !   This happy home :
  The darling at my knee !
My own dear wife !   Thyself, old Friend !
  And must it come to me
That any face shall fill my place
  Unknown to them and thee ?

RUSSET PITCHER.

"'The pot goeth so long to the water til at length it commeth broken home."

Away, ye simple ones, away!
    Bring no vain fancies hither;
The brightest dreams of youth decay,
    The fairest roses wither.

Ay, since this fountain first was planned,
    And Dryad learnt to drink,
Have lovers held, knit hand in hand,
    Sweet parley at its brink.

From youth to age this waterfall
    Most tunefully flows on,
But where, ay, tell me where are all
    The constant lovers gone?

The falcon on the turtle preys,
    And beardless vows are brittle;
The brightest dream of youth decays,—
    Ah, love is good for little.

"Sweet maiden, set thy pitcher down,
    And heed a Truth neglected :—
The more this sorry world is known,
    The less it is respected.

"Though youth is ardent, gay, and bold,
    It flatters and beguiles;
Though Giles is young, and I am old,
    Ne'er trust thy heart to Giles.

G 2

" Thy pitcher may some luckless day
   Be broken coming hither;
Thy doting slave may prove a knave,—
   The fairest roses wither."

She laughed outright, she scorned him quite,
   She deftly filled her pitcher;
For that dear sight an anchorite
   Might deem himself the richer.

Ill-fated damsel! go thy ways,
   Thy lover's vows are lither;
The brightest dream of youth decays,
   The fairest roses wither.

   *   *   *   *   *

These days were soon the days of yore;
   Six summers pass, and then
That musing man would see once more
   The fountain in the glen.

Again to stray where once he strayed,
   Through copse and quiet dell,
Half hoping to espy the maid
   Pass tripping to the well.

No light step comes, but, evil-starred,
    He finds a mournful token,—
There lies a russet pitcher marred,—
    The damsel's pitcher broken!

Profoundly moved, that muser cried,
    "The spoiler has been hither;
O would the maiden first had died,—
    The fairest rose must wither!"

He turned from that accursèd ground,
    His world-worn bosom throbbing;
A bow-shot thence a child he found,
    The little man was sobbing.

He gently stroked that curly head,—
    "My child, what brings thee hither?
Weep not, my simple one," he said,
    "Or let us weep together.

"Thy world, I ween, is gay and green
    As Eden undefiled;
Thy thoughts should run on mirth and fun,—
    Where dwellest thou, my child?"

'Twas then the rueful urchin spoke :—
" My daddy's Giles the ditcher,
I fetch the water,—and I've broke . . .
I've broke my mammy's pitcher!"

THE FAIRY ROSE.

" THERE are plenty of roses," (the patriarch speaks)
" Alas! not for me, on your lips, and your cheeks ;
Sweet maiden, rose-laden—enough and to spare,—
Spare, oh spare me the Rose that you wear in your
  hair."

" O raise not thy hand," cries the maid, " nor suppose
That I ever can part with this beautiful Rose :
The bloom is a gift of the Fays, who declare, it
Will shield me from sorrow as long as I wear it.

" ' Entwine it,' said they, ' with your curls in a braid,
It will blossom in winter—it never will fade ;
And, when tempted to rove, recollect, ere you hie,
Where you're dying to go—'twill be going to die.'

" And sigh not, old man, such a doleful ' heighho,'
Dost think I possess not the will to say ' No ? '
And shake not thy head, I could pitiless be
Should supplicants come more persuasive than thee."

The damsel passed on with a confident smile,
The old man extended his walk for awhile ;
His musings were trite, and their burden, forsooth,
The wisdom of age, and the folly of youth.

Noon comes, and noon goes, paler twilight is there,
Rosy day dons the garb of a penitent fair ;
The patriarch strolls in the path of the maid,
Where cornfields are ripe, and awaiting the blade.

And Echo was mute to his leisurely tread,—
" How tranquil is nature reposing," he said ;
He onward advances, where boughs overshade,
" How lonely," quoth he—and his footsteps he stayed !

He gazes around, not a creature is there,
No sound on the ground, and no voice in the air ;
But fading there lies a poor Bloom that he knows,
—Bad luck to the Fairies that gave her the Rose.

1863.

These verses were published in 1863, in " A Welcome," dedicated to the Princess of Wales.

THE town despises modern lays :
 The foolish town is frantic
For story-books which tell of days
 That time has made romantic :
Those days whose chiefest lore lies chill
 And dead in crypt and barrow ;
When soldiers were—as Love is still—
 Content with bow and arrow.

But why should we the fancy chide ?
 The world will always hunger
To know how people lived and died
 When all the world was younger.
We like to read of knightly parts
 In maidenhood's distresses :
Of trysts with sunshine in light hearts,
 And moonbeams on dark tresses ;

And how, when errant-*knyghte* or *erl*
   Proved well the love he gave her,
She sent him scarf or silken curl,
   As earnest of her favour;
And how (the Fair at times were rude!)
   Her knight, ere homeward riding,
Would take—and, ay, with gratitude—
   His lady's silver chiding.

We love the "rare old days and rich"
   That poesy has painted;
We mourn the "good old times" with which
   We never were acquainted.
Last night a lady tried to prove
   (And not a lady youthful):
"Ah, once it was no crime to love,
   Nor folly to be truthful!"

Absurd! Then dames in castles dwelt,
   Nor dared to show their noses:
Then passion that could not be spelt,
   Was hinted at in posies.
Such shifts make modern Cupid laugh:
   For sweethearts, in love's tremor,
Now tell their vows by telegraph—
   And go off in the steamer!

The earth is still our Mother Earth—
  Young shepherds still fling capers
In flowery groves that ring with mirth —
  Where old ones read the papers.
Romance, as tender and as true,
  Our Isle has never quitted :
So lads and lasses when they woo
  Are hardly to be pitied !

Oh, yes ! young love is lovely yet—
  With faith and honour plighted :
I love to see a pair so met—
  Youth—Beauty—all united.
Such dear ones may they ever wear
  The roses Fortune gave them :
Ah, know we such a Blessed Pair?
  I think we do !   GOD SAVE THEM !

Our lot is cast on pleasant days,
  In not unpleasant places—
Young ladies now have pretty ways,
  As well as pretty faces ;
So never sigh for what has been,
  And let us cease complaining
That we have loved when Our Dear Queen
  Victoria was reigning !

GERALDINE GREEN.

I.

THE SERENADE.

LIGHT slumber is quitting
  The eyelids it pressed,
The fairies are flitting,
  Who charmed thee to rest :
Where night-dews were falling
  Now feeds the wild bee,
The starling is calling,
  My Darling, for thee.

The wavelets are crisper
  That sway the shy fern,
The leaves fondly whisper,
  "We wait thy return."
Arise then, and hazy
  Distrust from thee fling,
For sorrows that crazy
  To-morrows may bring.

A vague yearning smote us—
    But wake not to weep,
My bark, love, shall float us
    Across the still deep,
To isles where the lotos,
    Erst lulled thee to sleep.

II.

MY LIFE IS A ——

AT Worthing an exile from Geraldine G——,
How aimless, how wretched an exile is he !
Promenades are not even prunella and leather
To lovers, if lovers can't foot them together.

He flies the parade, sad by ocean he stands,
He traces a " Geraldine G." on the sands,
Only " G !" though her loved patronymic is " Green,"—
I will not betray thee, my own Geraldine.

The fortunes of men have a time and a tide,
And Fate, the old Fury, will not be denied ;
That name was, of course, soon wiped out by the sea,—
She jilted the exile, did Geraldine G.

They meet, but they never have spoken since that,—
He hopes she is happy—he knows she is fat ;
She woo'd on the shore, now is wed in the Strand,—
And *I*—it was I wrote her name on the sand !

MRS. SMITH.

LAST year I trod these fields with Di,
And that's the simple reason why
    They now seem arid :
Then Di was fair and single—how
Unfair it seems on me—for now
    Di's fair, and married.

In bliss we roved.   I scorned the song
Which says that though young Love is strong
    The Fates are stronger:
Then breezes blew a boon to men—
Then buttercups were bright—and then
    This grass was longer.

That day I saw, and much esteemed
Di's ankles—which the clover seemed
    Inclined to smother:
It twitched, and soon untied (for fun)
The ribbons of her shoes—first one,
    And then the other.

'Tis said that virgins augur some
Misfortune if their shoestrings come
    To grief on Friday:
And so did Di—and so her pride
Decreed that shoestrings so untied,   ·
    " Are so untidy !"

Of course I knelt—with fingers deft
I tied the right, and then the left :
    Says Di—" This stubble
Is very stupid—as I live
I'm shocked—I'm quite ashamed to give
    You so much trouble."

For answer I was fain to sink
To what most swains would say and think
    Were Beauty present :
" Don't mention such a simple act—
A trouble ? not the least.   In fact
    It's rather pleasant."

I trust that love will never tease
Poor little Di, or prove that he's
    A graceless rover.
She's happy now as *Mrs. Smith*—
But less polite when walking with
    Her chosen lover.

Heigh-ho ! Although no moral clings
To Di's soft eyes, and sandal strings,
    We've had our quarrels !—
I think that Smith is thought an ass,
I know that when they walk in grass
    She wears balmorals.

THE SKELETON IN THE CUPBOARD.

THE characters of great and small
  Come ready made, we can't bespeak one;
Their sides are many, too,—and all
  (Except ourselves) have got a weak one.
Some sanguine people love for life—
  Some love their hobby till it flings them,—
And many love a pretty wife
  For love of the *éclat* she brings them !

We all have secrets—you have one
  Which may not be your charming spouse's,—
We all lock up a skeleton
  In some grim chamber of our houses;
Familiars who exhaust their days
  And nights in probing where our smart is,
And who, excepting spiteful ways,
  Are quiet, confidential " parties."

We hug the phantom we detest,
  We rarely let it cross our portals :
It is a most exacting guest,—
  Now are we not afflicted mortals?
Your neighbour Gay, that joyous wight,
  As Dives rich, and bold as Hector,
Poor Gay steals twenty times a-night,
  On shaking knees, to see his spectre.

Old Dives fears a pauper fate,
  And hoarding is his thriving passion ;
Some piteous souls anticipate
  A waistcoat straiter than the fashion.
She, childless, pines,—that lonely wife,
  And hidden tears are bitter shedding ;
And he may tremble all his life,
  And die,—but not of that he's dreading.

Ah me, the World ! how fast it spins !
  The beldams shriek, the caldron bubbles ;
They dance, and stir it for our sins,
  And we must drain it for our troubles.
We toil, we groan,—the cry for love
  Mounts upward from this seething city,
And yet I know we have above
  A FATHER, infinite in pity.

When Beauty smiles, when Sorrow weeps,
　　When sunbeams play, when shadows darken,
One inmate of our dwelling keeps
　　A ghastly carnival—but hearken !
How dry the rattle of those bones !—
　　The sound was not to make you start meant,—
Stand by ! Your humble servant owns
　　The Tenant of this Dark Apartment.

THE VICTORIA CROSS.

A LEGEND OF TUNBRIDGE WELLS.

SHE gave him a draught freshly drawn from the
    springlet,—
O Tunbridge, thy waters are bitter, alas !
But Love finds an ambush in dimple and ringlet,—
"Thy health, pretty maiden !"—he emptied the
    glass.

He saw, and he loved her, nor cared he to quit her,
    The oftener he came, why the longer he stayed ;
Indeed, though the spring was exceedingly bitter,
    We found him eternally pledging the maid.

A *preux chevalier*, and but lately a cripple,
    He met with his hurt where a regiment fell,
But worse was he wounded when staying to tipple
    A bumper to " Phœbe, the Nymph of the Well."

Some swore he was old, that his laurels were faded,
  All vowed she was vastly too nice for a nurse ;
But Love never looked on such matters as they did,—
  She took the brave soldier for better or worse.

And here is the home of her fondest election,—
  The walls may be worn but the ivy is green ;
And here has she tenderly twined her affection
  Around a true soldier who bled for his Queen.

See, yonder he sits, where the church flings its shadows ;
  What child is that spelling the epitaphs there ?
To that imp'its devout and devoted old dad owes
  New zest in thanksgiving—fresh fervour in prayer.

Ere long, ay, too soon, a sad concourse will darken
  The doors of that church, and that tranquil abode ;
His place then no longer will know him—but, hearken,
  The widow and orphan appeal to their God.

Much peace will be hers ! " If our lot must be lowly,
  Resemble thy father, though with us no more ;"
And only on days that are high or are holy,
  She will show him the cross that her warrior wore.

So taught, he will rather take after his father,
   And wear a long sword to our enemies' loss ;
Till some day or other he'll bring to his mother
   Victoria's gift—the Victoria Cross?

And still she'll be charming, though ringlet and dimple
   Perchance may have lost their peculiar spell ;
And at times she will quote, with complacency simple,
   The compliments paid to the Nymph of the Well.

And then will her darling, like all good and true ones,
   Console and sustain her,—the weak and the
      strong ;—
And some day or other two black eyes or blue ones
   Will smile on his path as he journeys along.

Wherever they win him, whoever his Phœbe,
   Of course of all beauties she must be the *belle*,
If at Tunbridge he chance to fall in with a Hebe,
   He will not fall out with a draught from the Well.

.

ST. GEORGE'S, HANOVER SQUARE.

Dans le bonheur de nos meilleurs amis nous trouvons souvent quelque
chose qui ne nous plaît pas entièrement.

SHE passed up the aisle on the arm of her sire,
A delicate lady in bridal attire,—
    Fair emblem of virgin simplicity;—
Half London was there, and, my word, there were few,
Who stood by the altar, or hid in a pew,
    But envied Lord Nigel's felicity.

O beautiful Bride, still so meek in thy splendour,
So frank in thy love, and its trusting surrender,
    Departing you leave us the town dim!
May happiness wing to thy bosom, unsought,
And Nigel, esteeming his bliss as he ought,
    Prove worthy thy worship,—confound him!

SORRENTO.

Sorrento, stella d'amore.—VINCENZO DA FILICAIA.

SORRENTO ! Love's Star ! Land
    Of myrtle and vine,
I come from a far land
    To kneel at thy shrine ;
Thy brows wear a garland,
    Oh, weave one for mine !

Thine image, fair city,
    Smiles fair in the sea,—
A youth sings a pretty
    Song, tempered with glee, —
The mirth and the ditty
    Are mournful to me.

Ah, sea boy, how strange is
    The carol you sing !
Let Psyche, who ranges
    The gardens of Spring,
Remember the changes
    December will bring.

MARCH, 1862.

JANET.

I SEE her portrait hanging there,
Her face, but only half as fair,
  And while I scan it,
Old thoughts come back, by new thoughts met—
She smiles.   I never can forget
  The smile of Janet.

A matchless grace of head and hand,
Can Art pourtray an air more grand?
  It cannot—can it?
And then the brow, the lips, the eyes—
You look as if you could despise
  Devotion, Janet.

I knew her as a child, and said
She ought to have inhabited
  A brighter planet:
Some seem more meet for angel wings
Than Mother Nature's apron strings,—
  And so did Janet.

She grew in beauty, and in pride,
Her waist was slim, and once I tried,
    In sport, to span it,
At Church, with only this result,
They threatened with *quicunque vult*
    Both me and Janet.

She fairer grew, till Love became
In me a very ardent flame,
    With Faith to fan it :
Alas, I played the fool, and she . . .
The fault of both lay much with me,
    But more with Janet.

For Janet chose a cruel part,—
How many win a tender heart
    And then trepan it !
She left my bark to swim or sink,
Nor seemed to care—and yet, I think,
    You liked me, Janet.

The old old tale ! you know the rest—
The heart that slumbered in her breast
    Was soft as granite :
Who breaks a heart, and then omits
To gather up its broken bits,
    Is heartless, Janet.

I'm wiser now—for when I curse
My Fate, a voice cries, " Bad or worse
    You must not ban it :
Take comfort, you are quits, for if
You mourn a Love, stark dead and stiff,
    Why so does Janet."

BÉRANGER.

CAST adrift on this sphere
　　Where my fellows were born,
None gave me a tear,
　　I was weakly—forlorn.

My plaint for their spurning
　　To heaven took wing,—
Sweet voices said, yearning,
　　"Sing, Little One, sing !"

My lot, as I rove,
　　Is to sing for the throng ;—
And will not they love
　　The poor Child for his song !

THE BEAR PIT.

WE liked the bear's serio-comical face,
As he lolled with a lazy, a lumbering grace;
Said Slyboots to me—(just as if *she* had none),
" Papa, let's give Bruin a bit of your bun."

Says I, " A plum bun might please wistful old Bruin,
For he can't eat the stone that the cruel boy threw in;
Stick *yours* on the point of mama's parasol,
And then he will climb to the top of the pole.

"Some bears have got two legs, some bears have got
        more,—
Be good to old bears if they've no legs or four:
Of duty to age you should never be careless,
My dear, I am bald—and I soon shall be hairless!

" The gravest aversion exists amongst bears
For rude forward persons who give themselves airs,

We know how some graceless young people were
      mauled
For plaguing a prophet, and calling him bald.

" Strange ursine devotion! Their dancing-days ended,
Bears die to ' remove' what, in life, they defended :
They succoured the Prophet, and since that affair
The bald have a painful regard for the bear."

My Moral—Small People may read it, and run,
(The child has my moral, the bear has my bun),—
Forbear to give pain, if it's only in jest,
And care to think pleasure a phantom at best.
A paradox too—none can hope to attach it,
Yet if you pursue it you'll certainly catch it.

THE CASTLE IN THE AIR.

You shake your curls, and wonder why
I build no Castle in the Sky;
You smile, and you are thinking too,
He's nothing else on earth to do.
It needs Romance, my Lady Fair,
To raise such fabrics in the air—
Ethereal brick, and rainbow beam,
The gossamer of Fancy's dream,

And much the architect may lack
Who labours in the Zodiac
To rear what I, from chime to chime,
Attempted once upon a time.

My Castle was a gay retreat
  In Air, that somewhat gusty shire,
A cherub's model country seat,—
  Could model cherub such require.
Nor twinge nor tax existence tortured,
The cherubs even spared my orchard !
No worm destroyed the gourd I planted,
And showers arrived when rain was wanted.
I owned a range of purple mountain—
A sweet, mysterious, haunted fountain—
A terraced lawn—a summer lake,
  By sun- or moon-beam always burnished ;
And then my cot, by some mistake,
  Unlike most cots, was neatly furnished.
A trellised porch—a pictured hall—
A Hebe laughing from the wall.
  Frail vases, Attic and Cathay.
While under arms and armour wreathed
In trophied guise, the marble breathed,
  A peering faun—a startled fay.
And flowers that Love's own language spoke,

Than these less eloquent of smoke,
And not so dear.   The price in town
Is half a rose-bud—half-a-crown !
And cabinets and chandeliers,
The legacy of courtly years ;
And missals wrought by hooded monks,
Who snored in cells the size of trunks,
And tolled a bell, and told a bead,
(Indebted to the hood indeed !)
Stained windows dark, and pillowed light,
Soft sofas, where the Sybarite
In bliss reclining, might devour
The best last novel of the hour.
On silken cushion, happy starred,
A shaggy Skye kept wistful guard :
While drowsy-eyed, would dozing swing
A parrot in his golden ring.

All these I saw one blissful day,
    And more than now I care to name ;
Here, lately shut, that work-box lay,
    There, stood your own embroidery frame.
And over this piano bent
A Form from some pure region sent.
Despair, some lively trope devise
To prove the splendour of her eyes !

Her mouth had all the rose-bud's hue—
A most delicious rose-bud too.
Her auburn tresses lustrous shone,
In massy clusters, like your own ;
And as her fingers pressed the keys,
How strangely they resembled these !

Yes, you, you only, Lady Fair,
Adorned a Castle in the Air,
Where life, without the least foundation,
Became a charming occupation.
We heard, with much sublime disdain,
The far-off thunder of Cockaigne ;
And saw, through rifts of silver cloud,
The rolling smoke that hid the crowd.
With souls released from earthly tether,
We hymned the tender moon together.
Our sympathy from night to noon
Rose crescent with that crescent moon ;
The night was shorter than the song,
And happy as the day was long.
We lived and loved in cloudless climes,
And even died (in verse) sometimes.

Yes, you, you only, Lady Fair,
Adorned my Castle in the Air.

Now, tell me, could you dwell content
In such a baseless tenement?
Or could so delicate a flower
Exist in such a breezy bower?
Because, if you would settle in it,
'Twere built for love, in half a minute.

What's love? Why love (for two) at best,
Is only a delightful jest;
But sad indeed for one or three,
—I wish you'd come and jest with me.

You shake your head and wonder why
   The cynosure of dear Mayfair
Should lend me even half a sigh
   Towards building Castles in the Air.
" I've music, books, and all you say,
To make the gravest lady gay.
I'm told my essays show research,
My sketches have endowed a church;
I've partners who have brilliant parts,
I've lovers who have broken hearts.
Poor Polly has not nerves to fly,
And why should Mop return to Skye?
To realize your *tête-à-tête*
Might jeopardize a giddy pate;

As grief is not akin to guilt,
I'm sorry if your Castle's built."

Ah me—alas for Fancy's flights
In noonday dreams and waking nights !
The pranks that brought poor souls mishap
When baby Time was fond of pap ;
And still will cheat with feigning joys,
While ladies smile, and men are boys.
The blooming rose conceals an asp,
And bliss, coquetting, flies the grasp.
How vain the prize that pleased at first !
But myrtles fade, and bubbles burst.
The cord has snapt that held my kite ;—
My friends neglect the books I write,
    And wonder why the author's spleeny !
I dance, but dancing's not the thing ;
They will not listen though I sing
    " Fra poco," almost like Rubini !
The poet's harp beyond my reach is,
The Senate will not stand my speeches,
I risk a jest,—its point of course
Is marred by some disturbing force ;
I doubt the friends that Fortune gave me ;
But have I friends from whom to save me ?

Farewell,—can aught for her be willed
Whose every wish is all fulfilled?
Farewell,—could wishing weave a spell,
There's promise in the word "farewell."

The lady's smile showed no remorse,—
    "My worthless toy hath lost its gilding,"
I murmured with pathetic force,
    "And here's an end of castle building;"
Then strode away in mood morose,
To blame the Sage of Careless Close,
He trifled with my tale of sorrow,—
"What's marred to-day is made to-morrow;
Romance can roam not far from home,
    Knock gently, she must answer soon;
I'm sixty-five, and yet I strive
    To hang my garland on the moon."

GLYCERE.

OLD MAN.

In gala dress, and smiling ! Sweet,
What seek you in my green retreat?

YOUNG GIRL.

I gather flowers to deck my hair,—
  The village yonder claims the best,
For lad and lass are thronging there
  To dance the sober sun to rest.
Hark ! hark ! the rebec calls,—Glycere
  Again may foot it on the green ;
Her rivalry I need not fear,
  These flowers shall crown the Village Queen.

OLD MAN.

You long have known this tranquil ground ?

YOUNG GIRL.

It all seems strangely marred to me.

OLD MAN.

Light heart! there sleeps beneath this mound
  The brightest of yon company.
The flowers that should eclipse Glycere
Are hers, poor child,—her grave is here!

VÆ VICTIS.

"My Kate, at the Waterloo Column,
  To-morrow, precisely at eight;
Remember, thy promise was solemn,
  And—thine till to-morrow, my Kate!"

    *   *   *   *   *

That evening seemed strangely to linger,—
  The licence and luggage were packed;
And Time, with a long and short finger,
  Approvingly marked me exact.

Arrived, woman's constancy blessing,
  No end of nice people I see;
Some hither, some thitherwards pressing,—
  But none of them waiting for me.

Time passes, my watch how I con it!
  I see her—she's coming—no, stuff!
Instead of Kate's smart little bonnet,
  It is aunt, and her wonderful muff!

(Yes, Fortune deserves to be chidden,
    It is a coincidence queer,
Whenever one wants to be hidden,
    One's relatives always appear.)

Near nine ! how the passers despise me,
    They smile at my anguish, I think ;
And even the sentinel eyes me,
    And tips that policeman the wink.

Ah ! Kate made me promises solemn,
    At eight she had vowed to be mine ;—
While waiting for one at this column,
    I find I've been waiting for nine.

O Fame ! on thy pillar so steady,
    Some dupes watch beneath thee in vain :—
How many have done it already !
    How many will do it again !

IMPLORA PACE.

ONE hundred years ! a long, long scroll
   Of dust to dust, and woe,
How soon my passing knell will toll !
   Is Death a friend or foe ?
My days are often sad—and vain
Is much that tempts me to remain
   —And yet I'm loth to go.
Oh, must I tread yon sunless shore—
Go hence, and then be seen no more ?

I love to think that those I loved
   May gather round the bier
Of him, who, whilst he erring proved,
   Still held them more than dear.
My friends wax fewer day by day,
Yes, one by one, they drop away,
   And if I shed no tear,

Dear parted Shades, whilst life endures,
This poor heart yearns for love—and yours !

Will some who knew me, when I die,
   Shed tears behind the hearse ?
Will any one survivor cry,
   " I could have spared a worse—
We never spoke : we never met :
I never heard his voice—and yet
   I loved him for his verse ?"
Such love would make the flowers wave
In rapture on their poet's grave.

One hundred years ! They soon will leak
   Away—and leave behind
A stone mossgrown, that none will seek,
   And none would care to find.
Then I shall sleep, and find release
In perfect rest—the perfect peace
   For which my soul has pined ;
Although the grave is dark and deep
I know the Shepherd loves his sheep.

VANITY FAIR.

" *VANITAS vanitatum* " has rung in the ears
Of gentle and simple for thousands of years ;
The wail is still heard, yet its notes never scare
Or simple or gentle from Vanity Fair.

I hear people busy abusing it—yet .
There the young go to learn and the old to forget ;
The mirth may be feigning, the sheen may be glare,
But the gingerbread's gilded in Vanity Fair.

Old Dives there rolls in his chariot, but mind
Atra Cura is up with the lacqueys behind ;
Joan trudges with Jack,—is his sweetheart aware
What troubles await them in Vanity Fair ?

We saw them all go, and we something may learn
Of the harvest they reap when we see them return ;
The tree was enticing,—its branches are bare,—
Heigh-ho, for the promise of Vanity Fair !

.

That stupid old Dives! forsooth, he must barter
His time-honoured name for a wonderful garter;
And Joan's pretty face has been clouded with care
Since Jack bought *her* ribbons at Vanity Fair.

Contemptible Dives! too credulous Joan!
Yet we all have a Vanity Fair of our own;—
My son, you have yours, but you need not despair.
Myself I've a weakness for Vanity Fair.

Philosophy halts, wisest counsels are vain,—
We go—we repent—we return there again;
To-night you will certainly meet with us there—
Exceedingly merry in Vanity Fair.

THE LEGENDE OF SIR GYLES GYLES.

Notissimum illud Phædri, *Gallus quum tauro*.

Uppe, lazie loon ! 'tis mornynge prime,
  The cockke of redde redde combe
This thrice hath crowed—'tis past the time
  To drive the olde bulle home.

Goe fling a rope about his hornnes,
  And lead him safelie here :
Long since Sir Gyles, who slumber scornes,
  Doth angle in the weir.

And, knaves and wenches, stay your din,
  Our Ladye is astir :
For hark and hear her mandolin
  Behynde the silver fir.

        o

His Spanish hat he bravelie weares,
  With feathere droopynge wide,
In doublet fyne, Sir Valentyne
  Is seated by her side.

Small care they share, that blissfulle pair ;
  She dons her kindest smyles ;
His songes invite and quite delighte
  The wyfe of old Sir Gyles.

But pert young pages point their thumbes,
  Her maids look glumme, in shorte
All wondere how the good Knyghte comes
  To tarrie at his sporte.

There is a sudden stir at last ;
    Men run—and then, with dread,
They vowe Sir Gyles is dying fast !
    And then—Sir Gyles is dead !

The bulle hath caughte him near the thornes
    They call the *Parsonne's Plotte ;*
The bulle hath tossed him on his hornnes,
    Before the brute is shotte.

Now Ladye Gyles is sorelie tryd,
    And sinks beneath the shockke :
She weeps from morn to eventyd,
    And then till crowe of cockke.

Again the sun returns, but though
    The merrie morninge smiles,
No cockke will crow, no bulle will low
    Agen for pore Sir Gyles.

And now the knyghte, as seemeth beste,
    Is layd in hallowed mould ;
All in the mynstere crypt, where rest
    His gallant sires and old.

K

But first they take the olde bulle's skin
    And crest, to form a shroud :
And when Sir Gyles is wrapped therein
    His people wepe aloud.

Sir Valentyne doth well incline
    To soothe my lady's woe ;
And soon she'll slepe, nor ever wepe,
    An all the cockkes sholde crowe.

Ay soone they are in wedlock tied,
    Full soon ; and all, in fyne,
That spouse can say to chere his bride,
    That sayth Sir Valentyne.

And gay agen are maids and men,
    Nor knyghte nor ladye mournes,
Though Valentyne may trembel when
    He sees a bulle with hornnes.

*   *   *   *   *

My wife and I once visited
    The scene of all this woe,
Which fell out (so the curate said)
    Four hundred years ago.

It needs no search to find a church
    Which all the land adorns,
We passed the weir, I thought with fear
    About the *olde bulle's hornnes.*

No cock then crowed, no bull there lowed,
    But, while we paced the aisles,
The curate told his tale, and showed
    A tablet to Sir Giles.

"'Twas raised by Lady Giles," he said,
    And when I bent the knee I
Made out his name, and arms, and read,
    HIC JACET SERVVS DEI.

Says I, "And so he sleeps below,
    His wrongs all left behind him."
My wife cried, "Oh!" the clerk said, "No,
    At least we could not find him.

" Last spring, repairing some defect,
    We raised the carven stones,
Designing to again collect
    And hide Sir Giles's bones.

Yet while it so pleased him to ponder,
　　Elated, at ease, and alone ;
That pale, patient victim up yonder
　　Had budding delights of her own ;

Sweet thoughts, in their essence diviner
　　Than paltry ambition and pelf ;
A cherub, no babe will be finer,
　　Invented and nursed by herself.

One breakfasting, dining, and teaing,
　　With appetite nought can appease,
And quite a young Reasoning Being
　　When called on to yawn and to sneeze.

What cares that heart, trusting and tender,
　　For fame or avuncular wills !
Except for the name and the gender,
　　She is almost as tranquil as Squills.

That father, in reverie centered,
　　Dumbfoundered, his thoughts in a whirl,
Heard Squills, as the creaking boots entered,
　　Announce that his Boy was—a Girl.

SUSANNAH.

I.

THE ELDER TREES.

AT Susan's name the fancy plays
With chiming thoughts of early days,
   And hearts unwrung ;
When all too fair our future smiled,
When she was Mirth's adopted child,
   And I was young.

I see the cot with spreading eaves,
The sun shines bright through summer leaves,
   But does not scorch,—
The dial stone, the pansy bed ;—
Old Robin trained the roses red
   About the porch.

'Twixt elders twain a rustic seat
Was merriest Susan's pet retreat
   To merry make ;

" We delvèd down, and up, and round,
    For many weary morns,
Through all this ground ; but only found
    An ancient pair of horns."

MY FIRST-BORN.

" HE shan't be their namesake, the rather
  That both are such opulent men :
His name shall be that of his father,—
  My Benjamin—shortened to Ben.

" Yes, Ben, though it cost him a portion
  In each of my relative's wills,
I scorn such baptismal extortion—
  (That creaking of boots must be Squills).

" It is clear, though his means may be narrow,
  This infant his age will adorn ;
I shall send him to Oxford from Harrow,—
  I wonder how soon he'll be born !"

A spouse thus was airing his fancies
  Below—'twas a labour of love,—
And calmly reflecting on Nancy's
  More practical labour above ;

Good Robin's handiwork again,—
Oh, must we say his toil was vain,
   For Susan's sake?

Her gleeful tones and laughter gay
Were sunshine for the darkest day;
   And yet, some said
That when her mirth was passing wild,
Though still the faithful Robin smiled,
   He shook his head.

Perchance the old man harboured fears
That happiness is wed with tears
   On this poor earth;
Or else, may be, his fancies were
That youth and beauty are a snare
   If linked with mirth.

*   *   *   *   *

And now how altered is that scene!
For mark old Robin's mournful mien,
   And feeble tread.
His toil has ceased to be his pride,
At Susan's name he turns aside,
   And shakes his head.

And summer smiles, but summer spells
Can never charm where sorrow dwells ;—
    No maiden fair,
Or gay, or sad, the passer sees,—
And still the much-loved Elder-trees
    Throw shadows there.

The homely-fashioned seat is gone,
And where it stood is set a stone,
    A simple square :
The worldling, or the man severe,
May pass the name recorded here ;
But we will stay to shed a tear,
    And breathe a prayer.

II.

A KIND PROVIDENCE.

He dropt a tear on Susan's bier,
   He seemed a most despairing swain ;
But bluer sky brought newer tie,
   And—would he wish her back again ?

The moments fly, and, when we die,
  Will Philly Thistletop complain?
She'll cry and sigh, and—dry her eye,
  And let herself be wooed again.

CIRCUMSTANCE.

THE ORANGE.

IT ripened by the river banks,
  Where, mask and moonlight aiding,
Dons Blas' and Juans play sad pranks,
  Dark Donnas serenading.

By Moorish maiden it was plucked,
  Who broke some hearts they say then :
By Saxon sweetheart it was sucked,
  —Who flung the peel away then.

How should she know in Pimlico
  Or t'other girl in Seville,
That *I* should reel upon that peel,
  And wish them at the Devil !

ARCADIA.

THE healthy-wealthy-wise affirm
That early birds secure the worm,
    (The worm rose early too!)
Who scorns his couch should glean by rights
A world of pleasant sounds and sights
    That vanish with the dew:

One planet from his watch released
Fast fading from the purple east,
    As morning waxes stronger;
The comely cock that vainly strives
To crow from sleep his drowsy wives,
    Who would be dozing longer.

Uxorious Chanticleer! and hark!
Upraise thine eyes, and find the lark,—
    The matutine musician
Who heavenward soars on rapture's wings,
Though sought, unseen,—who mounts and sings
    In musical derision.

From sea-girt pile, where nobles dwell,
A daughter waves her sire "farewell,"
    Across the sunlit water:
All these I heard, or saw—for fun
I stole a march upon that sun,
    And then upon that daughter.

This Lady Fair, the county's pride,
A white lamb trotting at her side,
    Had hied her through the park;
A fond and gentle foster-dam—
May be she slumbered with her lamb,
    Thus rising with the lark!

The lambkin frisked, the lady fain
Would coax him back, she called in vain,
        The rebel proved unruly ;
I followed for the maiden's sake,
A pilgrim in an angel's wake,
        A happy pilgrim truly !

The maid gave chase, the lambkin ran
As only woolly truant can
        Who never felt a crook ;
But stayed at length, as if disposed
To drink, where tawny sands disclosed
        The margin of a brook.

His mistress, who had followed fast,
Cried, " Little rogue, you're caught at last ;
        I'm cleverer than you."
Then straight the wanderer conveyed
Where wayward shrubs, in tangled shade,
        Protected her from view.

And timidly she glanced around,
All fearful lest the slightest sound
        Might mortal footfall be ;
Then shrinkingly she stepped aside
One moment—and her garter tied
        The truant to a tree.

Perhaps the World may wish to know
The hue of this enchanting bow,
　　And if 'twere silk or lace ;
No, not from me, be pleased to think
It might be either—blue or pink,
　　'Twas tied—with maiden grace.

Suffice it that the child was fair,
As Una sweet, with golden hair,
　　And come of high degree ;
And though her feet were pure from stain,
She turned her to the brook again,
　　And laved them dreamingly.

Awhile she sat in maiden mood,
And watched the shadows in the flood,
　　That varied with the stream ;
And as each pretty foot she dips,
The ripples ope their crystal lips
　　In welcome, as 'twould seem.

Such reveries are fleeting things,
Which come and go on whimsy wings,—
　　As kindly Fancy taught her
The Fair her tender day-dream nurst ;
But when the light-blown bubble burst,
　　She wearied of the water ;

Betook her to the spot where yet
Safe tethered lay her captured pet,
    But lifting, with a start, her
Astonished gaze, she spied a change,
And screamed—it seemed so very strange ! . .
    Cried Echo,—" Where's my garter ? "

The blushing girl her lamb led home,
Perhaps resolved no more to roam
    At peep of day together ;
If chance so takes them, it is plain
She will not venture forth again
    Without an extra tether !

A fair white stone will mark this morn,
I wear a prize, one lightly worn,
    Love's gage—though not intended—
·Of course I'll guard it near my heart.
Till suns and even stars depart,
    And chivalry has ended.

Dull World ! I now resign to you
Those crosses, stars, and ribbons blue,
    With which you deck your martyrs :
I'll bear my cross amid your jars,
My ribbon prize, and thank my stars
    I do not crave your garters.

THE CROSSING-SWEEPER.

AZLA AND EMMA.

A CROSSING-SWEEPER, black and tan,
Tells how he came from Hindostan,
And why he wears a hat, and shunned
The fatherland of Pugree Bund.

My wife had charms, she worshipped me,---
Her father was a Caradee,
His deity was aquatile,
A rough and tough old Crocodile.

To gratify this monster's maw
He sacrificed his sons-in-law ;
We married, tho' the neighbours said he
Had lost five sons-in-law already.

L

Her father, when he played these pranks,
Proposed "a turn" on Jumna's banks;
He spoke so kind, she seemed so glum,
I knew at once that mine had come.

I fled before this artful ruse
To cook my too-confiding goose,
And now I sweep, in chill despair,
This crossing in St. James's Square;

Some old *Qui-hy*, some rural flat
May drop a sixpence in my hat;
Yet still I mourn the mango-tree
Where Azla first grew fond of me.

These rogues, who swear my skin is tawny,
Would pawn their own for brandy-pawnee;
What matters it if theirs are snowy,
As Chloe fair! They're drunk as Chloe!

Your town is vile.   In Thames's stream
The crocodiles get up the steam!
Your juggernauts their victims bump
From Camberwell to Aldgate pump!

A year ago, come Candlemas,
I wooed a plump Feringhee lass;
United at her idol fane,
I furnished rooms in Idol Lane.

A moon had waned when virtuous Emma
Involved me in a new dilemma:
The Brahma faith that Emma scorns
Impaled me tight on both its horns:

She vowed to die if she survived me;
Of this sweet fancy she deprived me,
She ran from all her obligations,
And went to stay with her relations.

My Azla weeps by Jumna's deeps,
   But Emma mocks my trials,—
She pokes her jokes in Seven Oaks,
   At me in Seven Dials,—
She'd see me farther still, than be,
Though Veeshnu wills it—my *Suttee!*

A SONG THAT WAS NEVER SUNG.

THOU sayest our friends are only dead
  To idle mirth and sorrow,
Regretful tears for what is fled,
  And yearnings for to-morrow.
Alas, that love should know alloy—
How frail the cup that holds our joy !

Thou sighest, " How sweet it were to rove
  Those paths of asphodel ;
Where all we prize, and all who love,
  Rejoice !" Ah, who can tell?
Yet sweet it were, knit hand in hand,
To lead thee through a better land.

Why wish the fleeting years to stay?—
  When time for us is flown,
There is this garden,—far away,
  An Eden all our own :
And there I'll whisper in thine ear
—Ah ! what I may not tell thee here !

MR. PLACID'S FLIRTATION.

"Jemima was cross, and I lost my umbrella
That day at the tomb of Cecilia Metella."
Letters from Rome.

Miss Tristram's *poulet* ended thus: "Nota bene,
We meet for croquet in the Aldobrandini."
Says my wife, "Then I'll drive, and you'll ride with Selina,"
(The fair spouse of Jones, of the Via Sistina).

We started—I'll own that my family deem
That I'm soft—but I'm not quite so soft as I seem;
As we crossed the stones gently the nursemaids said
     "La!
There goes Mrs. Jones with Miss Placid's papa."

Our friends, some of whom may be mentioned anon,
Had made *rendezvous* at the Gate of St. John:
That passed, off we spun over turf that's not green
     there,
And soon were all met at the villa—you've been
     there?

I will try and describe, or I won't, if you please,
The cheer that was set for us under the trees:
You have read the *menu*, may you read it again,
Champagne, perigord, galantine, and—champagne.

Suffice it to say that, by chance, I was thrust
'Twixt Selina and Brown—to the latter's disgust.
Poor Brown, who believes in himself—and, another
     thing,
Whose talk is so bald, but whose cheeks are so—
     t'other thing.

She sang, her sweet voice filled the gay garden alleys;
I jested, but Brown would not smile at my sallies;
And Selina remarked that a swell met at Rome,
Is not always a swell when one meets him at home.

The luncheon despatched, we adjourned to croquet,
A dainty, but difficult sport, in its way.
Thus I counsel the Sage, who to play at it stoops,—
Belabour thy neighbour, and spoon through thy hoops.

Then we strolled, and discourse found its softest of
        tones:
"How charming were solitude and—Mrs. Jones."
"Indeed, Mr. Placid, I doat on these sheeny
And shadowy paths of the Aldobrandini."

A girl came with violet posies—and two
Soft eyes, like her violets, laden with dew;
And a kind of an indolent, fine-lady air,
As if she by accident found herself there.

I bought one.   Selina was pleased to accept it;
She gave me a rose-bud to keep—and I've kept it.
Thus the moments flew by, and I think, in my heart,
When one vowed one must go, two were loth to
        depart.

The twilight is near, we no longer can stay ;
The steeds are remounted, and wheels roll away.
The ladies *condemn* Mrs. Jones, as the phrase is,
But vie with each other in chanting my praises.

" He has so much to say," cries the fair Mrs. Legge ;
" How amusing he was about missing the peg !"
" What a beautiful smile !" says the plainest Miss
        Gunn.
All echo, " He's charming !   Delightful !   What
        fun !"

This sounds rather nice, and it's perfectly clear it
Would have sounded more nice if I'd happened to
        hear it ;
The men were less civil, and gave me a rub,
So I happened to hear when I went to the Club.

Says Brown, " I shall drop Mr. Placid's society ;"
But Brown is a prig of improper propriety.
" Confound him," says Smith (who from cant's not
        exempt),
" Why, he'll bring immorality into contempt."

Says I (to myself), when I found me alone,
" My wife has my heart, is it wholly her own ?"

And further, says I (to myself), " I'll be shot
If I know if Selina adores me or not."

Says Jones, " I've just come from the *scavi*, at Veii,
And I've bought some remarkably fine scarabœi."

TO PARENTS AND GUARDIANS.

PAPA was deep in weekly bills,
Mama was doing Fanny's frills,
    Her gentle face full
Of woe ; said she, " I do declare
He can't go back in such a Pair,
    They're too disgraceful ! "

" Confound it," quoth Papa—perhaps
The ban was deeper, but the lapse
    Of time has drowned it :
Besides, 'tis badness to suppose
A worse, when goodness only knows
    He meant *Confound it.*

The butcher's book—that unctuous diary—
Had made my Parent's temper fiery,
    And bubble over :
So quite in spite he flung it down,
And spilt the ink, and spoilt his own
    Fine table-cover

Of scarlet cloth !   Papa cried "pish !"
Which did not mean he did not wish
    He'd been more heedful :
"Good luck," said he, " this cloth will dip,
And make a famous pair—get Snip
    To do the needful."

'Twas thus that I went back to school
In garb no boy could ridicule,
    And eft becoming
A jolly child—I plunged in debt
For tarts—and promised fair to get
    The prize for summing.

But, no ! my schoolmates soon began
Again to mock my outward man,
    And make me hate 'em !
Long sitting will broadcloth abrade,
The dye wore off—and so displayed
    A red substratum !

To both my Parents then I flew—
Mama shed tears, Papa cried " Pooh,
    Come, stop this racket :"
He'd still some cloth, so Snip was bid
To stitch me on two tails ; he did,
    And spoilt my jacket !

And then the boys, despite my wails,
Would slily come and lift my tails,
    And smack me soundly.
O, weak Mama!   O, wrathful Dad!
Although your exploits drove me mad,
    Ye loved me fondly.

Good Friends, our little ones (who feel
Such bitter wounds, which only heal
    As wisdom mellows)
Need sympathy in deed and word ;
So never let them look absurd
    Beside their fellows.

My wife, who likes the Things I've doft,
Sublimes her sentiments, for oft,
    She'll take, and . . . air them !
—You little Puss, you love this pair,
And yet you never seem to care
    To let me wear them.

BEGGARS.

I am pacing Pall Mall in a wrapt reverie,—
I am thinking if Sophy is thinking of me,—
When up creeps a ragged and shivering wretch,
Who seems to be well on his way to Jack Ketch.

He has got a bad face, and a shocking bad hat,
A comb in his fist, and he sees I'm a flat ;
For he says, " Buy a comb, it's a fine un to wear ;
Just try it, my Lord, through your whiskers and 'air."

He eyes my gold chain, as if anxious to crib it ;
He looks just as if he'd been blown from a gibbet.
I pause . . . and pass on—and beside the club fire
I settle that Sophy is all I desire.

As I walk from the club, and am deep in a strophè,
Which rolls upon all that's delicious in Sophy,
I half tumble over an " object " unnerving—
So frightful a hag must be " highly deserving."

She begs—my heart's moved—but I've much circum-
        spection ;
I stifle remorse with the soothing reflection
That cases of vice are by no means a rarity—
The worst vice of all's indiscriminate charity.

Am I right? How I wish that our clerical guides
Would settle this question—and others besides !
For always to harden one's fiddlestrings thus,
If it's wholesome for beggars, is hurtful for us.

A few minutes later—how pleasant for me !—
I am seated by Sophy at five-o'clock tea :
Her table is loaded, for when a girl marries,
What cartloads of rubbish they send her from
        Barry's !

"There's a present for you !" Yes, my sweet Sophy's
        thrift
Has enabled the darling to buy me a gift.
And she slips in my hand—the delightfully sly Thing—
A paper-weight formed of a bronze lizard writhing.

"What a charming *cadeau !* and," says I, "so well
        made ;
But are you aware, you extravagant jade,

That in casting this metal a live, harmless lizard
Was cruelly tortured in ghost and in gizzard ? "

" Pooh, pooh," says my lady (I ought to defend her,
Her head is too giddy, her heart's much too tender),
" Hopgarten protests they've no feeling—and so
It was nothing but muscular movement, you know."

Thinks.I—when I've said *au revoir*, and depart—
(A Comb in my pocket, a Weight at my heart),—
And when wretched mendicants writhe, we've a notion
That begging is only a muscular motion.

The Angora Cat

GOOD pastry is vended
  In Cité Fadette,—
Madame Pons constructs splendid
  Brioche and *galette !*

Monsieur Pons is so fat that
  He's laid on the shelf,—
Madame Pons had a cat that
  Was fat as herself.

Long hair—soft as satin,—
　　A musical purr—
'Gainst the window she'd flatten
　　Her delicate fur.

Once I drove Lou to see what
　　Our neighbours were at,
When, in rapture, cried she, "What
　　An exquisite cat!　　·

"What whiskers!　She's purring
　　All over.　A gale
Of contentment is stirring
　　Her feathery tail.

"Monsieur Pons, will you sell her?"—
　　"*Ma femme est sortie,*
Your offer I'll tell her,
　　But—will she?" says he.

Yet Pons was persuaded
　　To part with the prize!
(Our bargain was aided,
　　My Lou, by your eyes!)

M

From his *légitime* save him—
My fate I prefer !
For I warrant she gave him
   Un mauvais quart d'heure.

I'm giving a pleasant
   Grimalkin to Lou,
—Ah, Puss, what a present
   I'm giving to you !

ON A PORTRAIT OF DR. LAURENCE
STERNE,

BY SIR JOSHUA REYNOLDS.

WHEN Punch gives friend and foe their due,
Can unwashed mirth grow riper?
Yet when the curtain falls, how few
Remain to pay the piper!

If pathos should thy bosom stir
To tears, more sweet than laughter,
Oh, bless its kind interpreter,
And love him ever after!

Dear Parson of the roguish eye!
Thy face has grown historic,
Since saint and sinner flocked to buy
The homilies of Yorick.

I fain would add one blossom to
   The chaplet Fame has wreathed thee.
My friends, the crew that Yorick drew
   Accept, as friends bequeathed thee.

At Shandy Hall I like to stop
   And see my ancient crony,
Or in the lane meet Dr. Slop
   Astride a slender pony.

Mine uncle, on his bowling-green,
   Still storms a breach in Flanders;
And faithful Trim, starch, tall, and lean,
   With Bridget still philanders.

And here again they visit us
   By happy inspiration,
The "fortunes of Pisistratus,"
   A tale of fascination.

But lay his magic volume by,
   And thank the Great Enchanter;—
Our loins are girded, let us try
   A sentimental canter. . . .

A Temple quaint of latest growth
　　Expands, where Art and Science
Astounded by our lack of both,
　　Have founded an alliance.

One picture there all passers scan,
　　It rivets friend and stranger :
Come, gaze on yonder guileless man,
　　And tremble for his danger.

Mine uncle's bluff—his waistcoat's buff,—
　　The heart beneath is tender,—
Bewitching widow !　Hold !　Enough !
　　Thou fairest of thy gender.

The limner's art !—the poet's pen !—
　　Posterity the story
Shall tell how these three gifted men
　　Have wrought for Yorick's glory.

O name not easily forgot !
　　Our love, dear Shade, we show thee,
Regretting thy misdeeds, but not
　　Forgetting what we owe thee.

A SKETCH IN SEVEN DIALS.

MINNIE, in her hand a sixpence,
  Toddled off to buy some butter;
(Minnie's pinafore was spotless)
  Back she brought it to the gutter,
Gleeful, radiant, as she thus did,
Proud to be so largely trusted.

One, two, three small steps she'd taken,
  Blissfully came little Minnie,
When, poor darling! down she tumbled,
  Daubed her hands and face and pinny!
Dropping too, the little slut, her
Pat of butter in the gutter.

Never creep back so despairing—
  Dry those eyes, my little fairy:
All of us start off in high glee,
  Many come back quite *contrairy*.
I've mourned sixpences in scores too,
Damaged hopes and pinafores too.

LITTLE PITCHER.

(A BIRTHDAY ODE.)

THE Muses, those painstaking Mentors of mine,
Observe that to-day Little Pitcher is nine!
'Tis her *fête*—so, although retrospection is pleasant,
While we muse on her Past, we must think of her
      Present.

A Gift!—In their praise she has raved, sung, and
    written,
Still, I don't seem to care for pup, pony, or kitten ;
Though their virtues I've heard Little Pitcher extol :
She's too old for a watch, and too young for a doll !

Of a worthless old Block she's the dearest of Chips,
For what nonsense she talks when she opens her lips.
Then her mouth—when she's happy—indeed, it
    appears
To laugh at the tips of her comical EARS.

Her Ears,—Ah, her Ears !—I remember the squallings
That greeted my own ears, when Rambert and
    Lawlings
Were boring (as I do) her Organs of Hearing—
Come, I'll give her for each of those Organs an Earring.

Here they are !   They are formed of the two scarabæi
That I bought of the old *contadino* at Veii.
They cost me some *pauls*, but, as history shows,
For what runs through the Ears, we must pay through
    the Nose.

And now, Little Pitcher, give ear to my rede,
And guard these two gems with a scrupulous heed,

For think of the woeful mishap that befel
The damsel who dropt her pair into a well.

That poor Little Pitcher would gladly have flown,
Or given her Ears to have let well alone ;
For when she got home her Instructress severe
Dismissed her to bed with a Flea in her Ear.

What? Tell you that tale? Come, a tale with a
      sting
Would be rather too much of an excellent thing !
I can't point a moral—or sing you the song—
My Years are too short—and your Ears are too long.

UNFORTUNATE MISS BAILEY.

(AN EXPERIMENT.)

WHEN he whispers, "O Miss Bailey,
　　Thou art brightest of the throng"—
She makes murmur, softly-gaily—
　　"Alfred, I have loved thee long."

Then he drops upon his knees, a
　　Proof his heart is soft as wax:
She's—I don't know who, but he's a
　　Captain bold from Halifax.

Though so loving, such another
　　Artless bride was never seen,
Coachee thinks that she's his mother
　　—Till they get to Gretna Green.

There they stand, by him attended,
  Hear the sable smith rehearse
That which links them, when 'tis ended,
  Tight for better—or for worse.

Now her heart rejoices—ugly
  Troubles need disturb her less—
Now the Happy Pair are snugly
  Seated in the night express.

So they go with fond emotion,
  So they journey through the night—
London is their land of Goshen—
  See, its suburbs are in sight !

Hark ! the sound of life is swelling,
  Pacing up, and racing down,
Soon they reach her simple dwelling—
  Burley Street, by Somers Town.

What is there to so astound them ?
  She cries " Oh ! " for he cries " Hah ! "
When five brats emerge, confound them !
  Shouting out, " Mama !—PAPA !"

While at this he wonders blindly,
  Nor their meaning can divine,
Proud she turns them round, and kindly,
  " All of these are mine and thine ! "

*   *   *   *   *

Here he pines, and grows dyspeptic,
  Losing heart he loses pith—
Hints that Bishop Tait's a sceptic—
  Swears that Moses was a myth.

Sees no evidence in Paley—
  Takes to drinking ratifia :
Shies the muffins at Miss Bailey
  While she's pouring out the tea.

One day, knocking up his quarters,
  Poor Miss Bailey found him dead,
Hanging in his knotted garters,
  Which she knitted ere they wed.

ADVICE TO A POET.

DEAR Poet, never rhyme at all !—
　　But if you must, don't tell your neighbours ;
Or five in six, who cannot scrawl,
　　Will dub you donkey for your labours.
This epithet may seem unjust
　　To you—or any verse-begetter :
Oh, must we own—I fear we must !—
　　That nine in ten deserve no better.

Then let them bray with leathern lungs,
　　And match you with the beast that grazes,—
Or wag their heads, and hold their tongues,
　　Or damn you with the faintest praises.
Be patient—you will get your due
　　Of honours, or humiliations :
So look for sympathy—but do
　　Not look to find it from relations.

When strangers first approved my books
  My kindred marvelled what the praise meant,
They now wear more respectful looks,
  But can't get over their amazement.
Indeed, they've power to wound, beyond
  That wielded by the fiercest hater,
For all the time they are so fond—
  Which makes the aggravation greater.

Most warblers now but half express
  The threadbare thoughts they feebly utter :
If they attempted nought—or less !
  They would not sink, and gasp, and flutter.
Fly low, my friend, then mount, and win
  The niche, for which the town's contesting ;
And never mind your kith and kin—
  But never give them cause for jesting.

A bard on entering the lists
  Should form his plan, and, having conn'd it,
Should know wherein his strength consists,
  And never, never go beyond it.
Great Dryden all pretence discards,
  Does Cowper ever strain his tether ?
And Praed—(Watteau of English Bards)—
  How well he keeps his team together !

Hold Pegasus in hand—control
   A vein for ornament ensnaring,
Simplicity is still the soul
   Of all that Time deems worth the sparing.
Long lays are not a lively sport,
   Reduce your own to half a quarter,
Unless your Public thinks them short,
   Posterity will cut them shorter.

I look on Bards who whine for praise,
   With feelings of profoundest pity :
They hunger for the Poets' bays
   And swear one's spiteful when one's witty.
The critic's lot is passing hard—
   Between ourselves, I think reviewers,
When called to truss a crowing bard,
   Should not be sparing of the skewers.

We all—the foolish and the wise—
   Regard our verse with fascination,
Through asinine paternal eyes,
   And hues of Fancy's own creation ;
Then pray, Sir, pray, excuse a queer
   And sadly self-deluded rhymer,
Who thinks his beer (the smallest beer !)
   Has all the gust of *alt hochheimer*.

Dear Bard, the Muse is such a minx,
   So tricksy, it were wrong to let her
Rest satisfied with what she thinks
   Is perfect : try and teach her better.
And if you only use, perchance,
   One half the pains to learn that we, Sir,
Still use to hide our ignorance—
   How very clever you will be, Sir !

NOTES.

Note to "A Human Skull."

"In our last month's Magazine you may remember there were some verses about a portion of a skeleton. Did you remark how the poet and present proprietor of the human skull at once settled the sex of it, and determined off-hand that it must have belonged to a woman? Such skulls are locked up in many gentlemen's hearts and memories. Bluebeard, you know, had a whole museum of them—as that imprudent little last wife of his found out to her cost. And, on the other hand, a lady, we suppose, would select hers of the sort which had carried beards when in the flesh."—*The Adventures of Philip on his Way through the World. Cornhill Magazine, January,* 1861.

Note to "An Invitation to Rome."

"He never sends a letter to her, but he begins a new one on the same day. He can't bear to let go her kind little hand as it were. He knows that she is thinking of him, and longing for him far away in Dublin yonder."—*English Humourists of the Eighteenth Century.*

Note to "To My Mistress."

"M. Deschanel quotes the following charming little poem, by Corneille, addressed to a young lady who had not been quite civil to him. He says with truth—'Le sujet est léger, le rhythme court, mais on y retrouve la fierté de l'homme, et aussi l'ampleur du tragique.' The verses are probably new to our readers. They are well worth reading :—

Marquise, si mon visage
A quelques traits un peu vieux,
Souvenez-vous, qu'à mon âge
Vous ne vaudrez guère mieux.

Le temps aux plus belles choses
Se plaît à faire un affront,
Et saura faner vos roses
Comme il a ridé mon front.

Le même cours des planètes
Règle nos jours et nos nuits ;
On m'a vu ce que vous êtes,
Vous serez ce que je suis.

Cependant j'ai quelques charmes
Qui sont assez éclatants
Pour n'avoir pas trop d'alarmes
De ces ravages du temps.

Vous en avez qu'on adore,
Mais ceux que vous méprisez
Pourraient bien durer encore
Quand ceux-là seront usés.

Ils pourront sauver la gloire
Des yeux qui me semblent doux,
Et dans mille ans faire croire
Ce qu'il me plaira de vous.

Chez cette race nouvelle
Où j'aurai quelque crédit,
Vous ne passerez pour belle
Qu'autant que je l'aurai dit.

Pensez-y, belle Marquise,
Quoiqu'un grison fasse effroi,
Il vaut qu'on le courtise
Quand il est fait comme moi.

The last four stanzas in particular are brimful of spirit, and the mixture of pride and vanity which they display is so remarkable that it seems impossible that it should have ever occurred in more than one person."—*Saturday Review, July 23rd*, 1864.

Note to "The Rose and the Ring."

MR. THACKERAY spent a portion of the winter of 1854 in Rome, and while there he wrote his little Christmas story called "The Rose and the Ring." He was a great friend of the distinguished American sculptor, Mr. Story, and was a frequent visitor at his house. I have heard Mr. Story speak with emotion of the kindness of Mr. Thackeray to his little daughter, then recovering from a severe illness, and he told me that Mr. Thackeray used to come nearly every day to read to Miss Story, often bringing portions of his manuscript with him.

Five or six years afterwards Miss Story showed me a very pretty copy of "The Rose and the Ring," which Mr. Thackeray had sent her, with a facetious sketch of himself in the act of presenting her with the work.

Note to "Béranger."

JETÉ sur cette boule,
  Laid, chétif, et souffrant;
Étouffé dans la foule,
  Faute d'être assez grand;

Une plainte touchante
  De ma bouche sortit;
Le bon Dieu me dit : Chante,
  Chante, pauvre petit !

Chanter, ou je m'abuse,
Est ma tâche ici-bas.
Tous ceux qu'ainsi j'amuse,
Ne m'aimeront-ils pas?

NOTE TO "GLYCÈRE."

Un Vieillard. JEUNE fille au riant visage,
Que cherches-tu sous cet ombrage?
La Jeune Fille. Des fleurs pour orner mes cheveux.
Je me rends au prochain village.
Avec le printemps et ses feux,
Bergères, bergers amoureux
Vont danser sur l'herbe nouvelle.
Déjà le sistre les appelle :
Glycère est sans doute avec eux.
De ces hameaux c'est la plus belle ;
Je veux l'effacer à leurs yeux :
Voyez ces fleurs, c'est un présage.
Le Vieillard. Sais-tu quel est ce lieu sauvage ?
La Jeune Fille. Non, et tout m'y semble nouveau.
Le Vieillard. Là repose, jeune étrangère,
La plus belle de ce hameau.
Ces fleurs pour effacer Glycère
Tu les cueilles sur son tombeau !

BÉRANGER.

BRADBURY AND EVANS, PRINTERS, WHITEFRIARS.